SEEING HER PAIN

HART SISTERS: BOOK ONE

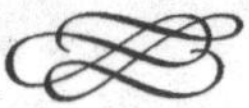

ALIE GARNETT

Edited by Thoth Editing

Image © DepositPhotos – Hay Dmittriy

Cover Design © Designed_with_Grace

❀ Created with Vellum

For my Family, without whom this series wouldn't have taken place on a farm in Minnesota.

CHAPTER 1

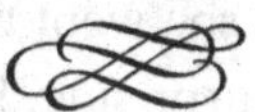

ACROSS THE BAR a full-blown fight broke out so suddenly, Gabe Watson hadn't even noticed it was brewing. There had been nothing unusual about the early evening crowd, and he barely glanced at the Lobo locals as they had trickled in. He silently cursed himself as he watched someone take a swing—he was supposed to be good at assessing danger.

Still chewing on a French fry, Gabe leapt off his stool at the bar, grabbing the shoulder of the short young soldier who had already sent two Jensen boys to the ground and was working on another.

Admittedly, he was impressed with how fast the soldier in Army greens had downed two men double her size, but Gabe needed to stop this fight *now*. The soldier whirled around on Gabe, trying to sweep his legs out from under him. She was in full attack mode. Just the tip of her pink tongue was visible as she concentrated on the battle. But it was the long lashes and gorgeous dark eyes that had him off guard and would have had him on the floor if not for the twenty plus years of service as a marine under his belt. This wasn't the first soldier to try these moves on him, and he was glad his training hadn't been lost this past year as a small-town cop.

The woman was small, and she was fighting with everything she had in her. Seeing how she had taken down two of the town's biggest bullies so quickly, he knew she could have taken all four of the brothers if she had enough time. She had picked up quite a few moves during her time in the service, but he was able to sidestep her fist as it flew towards him, missing his face by inches. Her dark brown eyes widened in surprise at missing the punch, sending her off balance and to the floor fast.

Gabe grabbed her waist as she went down, pulling her to him in an effort to make her stop. Not surprising, her instinct was to fight to get free from him and his tight hold of her. Once in his arms, he could hear her mumbling to herself, barely audible.

Movement caught his eye as he saw that one of the fallen Jensen boys was almost back on his feet and not too happy with the spitfire. The two still standing were heading his way, and being a cop wasn't going to be enough to stop them tonight. He grinned when he saw one of the boys still on the floor, out cold. *Good job soldier*.

Throwing her over his shoulder, he headed for the door to get her away from this mess and out of the bar. With any luck, the cold air would calm her down. As he walked to the door, she began pounding on his back and yelling at him to put her down. She even yelled at the bartender to call the cops. The corner of Gabe's mouth twitched up in response—did she even realize he was a cop? She was lighter than he had expected, but her warm body pressing against his felt good, even if she was using every move she knew to get off his shoulder. Maybe he needed to think about dating more if just touching a woman was having this effect on him.

The yelling and pounding on his back stopped as soon as the bar door closed behind them. The crisp evening air must have brought her back to her senses, because she had gone perfectly still. Had she passed out?

Lobos was on Main Street, and he had parked nearly a block from the door, even though the place was almost dead. The place needed a parking lot, desperately. With a huff, he hefted the soldier a little higher and headed down the road.

He didn't think she had been drinking—her movements would have been slower if she had been toasted, but she remained still as a rag doll on his shoulder. After walking about half a block from the bar, she asked quietly from his backside, "Where are you taking me?" The voice sounded small and more docile than he had expected, given that she had tried to punch him not two minutes before.

"Jail," he said firmly. "Fighting in a public place is a crime. And so is assaulting an officer." Gabe didn't really know what he was planning to do with the spitfire now that she was no longer *spitting fire*. The Jensen boys probably deserved everything she had given them. One of them was usually in a jail cell by Sunday morning, as it was.

"The jail's in the other direction. Are you going to carry me the entire way? That would be a first, being literally carried off to jail." She was making jokes, and she had to be a local… or at least used to be. He hadn't seen her around before, not that he had gotten a good look at her face, and wondered who she could be. He was sure he would have heard about a young female from this town serving in the Army.

"You're right, but my cruiser is this way. Are you going to try to punch a cop again if I put you down? Add another misdemeanor to your record?" He stopped by his patrol SUV, balancing the woman while reaching in his pocket for his keys with one hand.

He heard and felt her sigh, and then she mumbled into his back. "Probably. Just add it to my rap sheet."

"What?" He questioned sternly.

"No, no, I'll be good. I swear." Her words were clearer this time.

As if they had done this move a hundred times, she grabbed his shoulder and pushed her upper body upright as he slid her lower body slowly down to the pavement. He knew he'd made a mistake when he felt her entire solid little body against his. She had more curves than the unflattering uniform showed, and he had just brushed them *all* with his body—nice curves that he should not be noticing at all.

The hat she had been wearing had been lost somewhere between the bar and his cruiser, and now a street light was bouncing off the most amazing red curls Gabe had ever seen. Deep brown eyes were looking up at him—did she even know her hat was gone? Her shoulder-length ringlets were absolutely everywhere, just a mess, just…adorable.

Now that he saw the uncontrolled curls, he couldn't believe they had been contained in an Army-issued hat. He certainly hadn't noticed them during the fight. If he had, she probably would have landed that punch. As he gazed at her under the streetlight, the scent of ripe apples assaulted his senses, begging him to bury his face in the mass of curls. When he finally tore his eyes from her hair, he looked back into her eyes that were twinkling in the streetlight. Her pink lips curved into a slight, knowing smile, and the energy that radiated from her made him feel every bit of his nearly forty years.

"Hi." It was all he managed to say past the lump in his throat.

Her smile widened even more, and her hands were resting against his chest, fingers splayed. "Hi yourself."

She was still standing with her body pressed to his. He couldn't bring himself to break the contact, and she didn't seem to be going anywhere either. Clearing his throat, he asked, "Corporal Connor Hart, are you from around here?" He knew her grade and name by the patches on her uniform.

"Not a Corporal anymore, officer," she stated quietly, her smile vanishing as she looked at her arm, hands still resting on his. Her eyes then lit up again, and she said, "You bet I am. Born here, raised here, the whole shebang."

"Just getting out then?" Not that her previous answer didn't already tell him that.

"Yup, eight years and done." Shifting her stance so that they were even somehow closer, she asked, "How about you, Officer?"

Gabe tried not to enjoy the feel of her body on his. "Why do you think I was in the military?"

"They don't teach that kind of fighting in cop school." Her right hand began tapping his chest with each word she said. Was she flirting with him?

"Marines, twenty years. Been out for just over a year now." Gabe tried to emphasize the 'twenty years' part so she would get the point— he was old. Too old for her to be flirting with him, at least.

"*Marines*," she scoffed and stopped tapping. "You wasted your time in the marines. Everyone knows the Army is where the action's at."

Gabe managed to pull her hard, little body closer. He lowered his head and whispered in her ear, "Why be a grunt when you can be a Marine?"

She laughed at his joke. The sound made Gabe's heart do a flip in his chest. This woman was unlike any soldier he had ever known, and he had known quite a few. Hell, she was unlike any woman he had ever known. She was openly flirting with him in the middle of Main Street, having just met him less than ten minutes before. All he wanted to do was stay here with her forever. Learn everything there was to know about her.

They were still standing next to his cruiser with their bodies touching, his hands now resting on her round hips. Slowly, he slipped his hand around to her back and drew her hips a little closer. They were pressed, and he would only have to lower his head to kiss her sweet mouth. The mouth in question had a teasing grin on it that he wanted to taste. "What's your first name, Connor Hart?"

She was watching his mouth, and her breath caught at her name. "Connor Hart. I mean, Zoey. Zoey Connor Hart."

"Welcome home, Zoey Connor Hart," he said lazily, aware that they were still in the street in the middle of town. He liked her name. "Do you want a police escort home?" Had he just dropped a pickup line on her? *Really??* He was an idiot and was supposed to be working.

"Thanks for the offer, Officer, but been there and done that." Her eyes fluttered shut as she bit down hard on her soft pink lip.

Holding back a curse, because he wanted to be the one biting her lip. "Been taken home by a lot of cops, Zoey Connor Hart?" He chuckled, trying to lighten the mood, but the sparkle in her eyes had suddenly dimmed.

"Almost every one of them at some point, Officer. This isn't the first fight on my rap sheet," Smiling again as her hands slipped up his chest to connect behind his neck, she added, "It *was* the first time I missed while punching a cop, though. I've never missed before."

A groan slipped past his lips as her fingers brush the back of his neck. He had to focus. "How many other cops have you punched?"

"Before I answer that, I need to know your name, Officer, so I can add it to that long, long list." She was teasing him.

"Gabe."

"Gabe, as in short for Gabriel? Like the Angel?" She purred, still lightly running her fingers up and down his neck, causing lightning to run down his spine. His entire body had been on high alert since he touched her the first time, and her touches were not helping.

"I guess, but I'm no angel—just Gabe." He grinned. It was true, he was no angel, and he was thinking devilish thoughts about her right now.

Watching, he saw her eyes lower to read the name stitched into his shirt. Her brown eyes went wide, and the kissable grin she had had a moment ago was gone. Suddenly, she was mad as a hornet again. Pulling her arms away from him, she walked backwards until she hit his car.

"Gabriel Watson, the Marine. Of *course*, you are," she hissed and ran her fingers through the red curls, pulling them straight, then letting them bounce back in her anger.

"Do I know you?" He racked his mind for any Connor or Hart he might have ever known, but nothing came to him. He knew he had never seen this woman in his life. There's no way he would've forgotten that hair.

Stomping back up to him, she kept her eyes on his name tag, and with all her might, she pushed him away from her, sending him back a step. Then she took another full step at him and pushed him again just as hard. With one last glare, she turned and stomped away down the road.

"What did I do?" He called after her, his body already cold and missing her touch.

He watched as she spun around in the road and yelled, "You ran off with my mother; that's what you did!" Then she turned on her heels and headed down Main Street towards the bar he had just hauled her out of, but he could not move because he had no idea what she was talking about.

CHAPTER 2

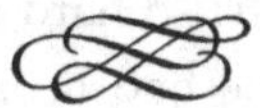

Zoey Hart stomped away from the sexy blue-eyed officer who had gotten her out of the jam with the Jensen boys at the bar. Though she could still feel his body pressed against hers, she hoped he wouldn't follow her. Right now, she was ready for a fight, and this time, she was sure to get arrested. Maybe the better thing would be to crawl back into his arms and never let go. Shaking her head, she had no idea what she would do if he came too close. Why was the man who she had instantly been drawn to the same one who ran off with her mother? It had been a long time since she had even wanted a man to *touch* her, but she had wanted this one to touch her…all over.

This was the first time she had ever even seen Gabriel Watson, the Marine, who had taken her mother away from her twenty years before. It was all she knew about the man, and it had always been enough.

Her mother had been gone by the time Zoey turned seven, never looking back at the family she had left behind. It had affected all three of the little girls that had to grow up without the mother that they needed. It had also left her dad a shell of a man who never recovered and died earlier in life than he should have.

Passing the door to the Lobo, she looked at the now-closed door. Stopping at her hometown bar had been a no-brainer since she had spent more time dreaming about their burgers than she did about coming home over the years. Knowing she would be driving past on her way to her sister Evie's house, she had to stop.

Everything had been great until the Jensen brothers showed up—all four of them. They were bigger than they had been eight years ago when she had last encountered them. The little one was an adult now, and the last time she had lived in town, he was fourteen. Back then, she had kicked him in the balls so hard it probably took another year for them to drop again, but he had been bullying a neighbor kid for most of the year and had deserved it. It wasn't the first time, but she had wanted to make sure it was the last. A few weeks later, she was in the army.

Maybe she should have left when they walked in, but we did not do her eating yet. Joey had been the one to start something, after all. Something about being stupid to fight in a war, so she had gone off on him. The other three joined in, and she really thought she could've handled them. Then suddenly, she was fighting with a cop! She hadn't even noticed a cop in the bar.

She wished she had gotten in a few more punches on Jeff and Jason —they deserved it for all the stuff they pulled on her back in high school—but two out of four was pretty good. This hadn't been the first time they had ganged up on her, and most likely wouldn't be the last. It was probably best to avoid the brothers for the next few weeks, which wouldn't be an issue since she'd planned on avoiding town altogether.

Next time, Officer Hunk wouldn't be there to haul her away. *No*, she thought, *Officer Stole-Thy-Mother*.

Why did Gabe Watson have to have the bluest eyes she had ever seen, and blond hair styled so perfectly that she wanted to mess it up just to see if he got mad? The feel of his body against hers as she slid down it was so hard, sexy, and perfect. But what puzzled her the most was that her world had been off-balance for months now, and once he picked her up in the bar, everything had righted itself, and she could think clearly again.

With a sigh, she leaned against her sister's car, second-guessing almost every decision she'd made in the last couple of hours. What was going on with her? She finally gets her mind clear only to try jumping the first guy she sees? She wasn't even the type to jump a man. In the dating game, she was more of a jumpee. But for a moment she had almost kissed him, not the other way around. She wasn't acting like herself at all.

Groaning, Zoey looked back to where she had left him by his patrol car, wanting one more glimpse of him, all tall and sexy with his blonde hair perfectly styled? But he wasn't a block away anymore he was walking towards her. And he was getting closer, close enough that she could tell he wasn't happy with her; gone was the sexy smirk.

Spinning back to the car, she fumbled for her keys. Jumping into the gray sedan, she took off before he could catch her. Ignoring the urge to stop and talk to him again, she hit the gas hard and peeled out of her parking spot. Then watched in her rear-view mirror as he simply stopped and stood in the middle of Main Street, staring after her.

Oh, great… Now I can add fleeing from a cop as my latest crime.

It took only ten minutes to drive the seven miles out of Birch Cove to get to the farm where she had been raised. Even though she'd been in the Army and seen the world for the past eight years, this little piece of land had always been home for her. Turning into the narrow gravel driveway, she saw that the house was mostly dark, only lit by the yard light and a dim light coming from the barn. Parking, she turned off the engine and let the silence engulf her. Slowly, she got out of the car—Della's car. Her oldest sister had let her borrow it for a few days, since she could get a ride to work. Thankfully, her sister had let her use the car, so middle sister Evie didn't have to come into the city to pick her up at the airport. But now Zoey and Evie would have to bring the car back as soon as they could.

The familiar house she'd been raised in looked lonely and neglected in the moonlight. Nobody lived here anymore. Evie and her son lived across the field in a house their dad had given them when her high school boyfriend had gotten her pregnant during their first semester of college. The boyfriend then became the husband, and within two years, he had killed himself, leaving her sister and their son behind.

Zoey still hated her brother-in-law for that. At twenty-one years old, he had already been a bitter drunk who couldn't get past the fact that he wasn't good enough to play football in college and had taken it out on anyone around him.

Zoey half expected to see her dad walk out the door, telling her she was late for curfew or that the principal had called...again. She had spent most of her time here grounded for something or another. Instead, the man was gone and had been for five years now. He'd had a heart attack after church on a Sunday afternoon, and she had barely been able to get leave to attend the funeral. They even made her ship out again the day after it was over.

But now she was home for good; home to farm the land like her dad had. She had spent the last eight years wanting to come back and farm with her dad. Evie had farmed with him for years, but when their dad had passed, Evie had insisted Zoey was not needed, so she reenlisted. Zoey hoped that there was enough room on the farm for both of them because there was simply nowhere else she wanted to go. Her soldiering days were over, and she was finally going to be a farmer.

With a sigh, she got back into the car and headed to Evie's house down the road. It had been her dad's parents' home before them. Grandparents that had been long gone before she had even been born.

Zoey was the baby and the wild one of the three. Evie was the second oldest and sort of became their mother figure, even though Della was older. The three of them weren't as close as they should've been, especially since Zoey had been gone for years. Della and Evie lived a few hours apart, and there had been a few short visits and phone calls, texts, and letters over the years, but nothing that had brought them closer. At this point, Zoey and her sisters were practically strangers.

Evie's farmhouse was lit up when Zoey drove into the yard. Her home always felt warm and lived-in, even though she and her son Ben had lived there alone. As far as she knew, Evie hadn't dated since being widowed ten years before, claiming that she was too busy making the farm a success. Zoey just hoped there was room for her in the operation.

The front door flew open before Zoey could get her seat belt off and the driver's door open. Her sister Evie ran out of the house, looking the same as she had for years. Evie never changed. As always, she had the same long blond hair in a braid and was wearing jeans and a flannel button-up shirt. With a smile Zoey leaping out the car to be enveloped in her sister's strong arms. The warm hug made Zoey feel welcome, and she hoped that Evie would see she had changed since high school. That she was no longer that crazy kid who had left here years before to join the Army. That Zoey was gone, hopefully forever.

CHAPTER 3

GABE WATCHED CORP. Zoey Connor Hart's hips sway as she walked back towards the Lobo. Still feeling her in his arms, he wished her body was still pressed against his. Following her in case she went back into the bar, Gabe let out a sigh of relief when she and her hips swayed past the Lobo to a car parked down the street. Her red curls bathed in streetlight he continued her way when she didn't get into the car, just leaned against the driver's door. Before he got too close, she spun and jumped into the car, and sped off. He stayed in the roadway until her taillights disappeared into the night, wondering why she had affected him so much in such a short amount of time.

Shaking his head, Gabe went back into the Lobo to pay his bill, even though he didn't have to. The bartender would have saved it for the next time he went in for a burger—this wasn't the first time one of his meals had been disrupted. Unfortunately, he was going to be on patrol for the rest of the night, so he went back in to kill a little time. The night shift was notoriously long and boring in Birch Cove.

The bar was back to its usual calm, quiet atmosphere. The Jensen boys were at the back table, nursing their wounds. Gabe noticed two had fat lips, and another was holding a beer to his eye. Josh seemed unaffected by the fight, but he wasn't moving too much. Last time he'd seen him, he had been on the ground. *She had gotten them good*, Gabe thought. They were nothing but trouble in this town. Then he noticed a crumpled hat on the floor near their table.

Walking up to the four young men, he bent and picked up Zoey's hat before asking, "What was the fight about?"

None of them were talking. They all seemed to be very interested in their beer bottle labels.

"Four against one, boys. And fighting a girl, too." He prodded, crossing his arms over his chest.

"Zoey Hart deserves everything she gets, Watson. You should arrest her." Josh said from behind the beer bottle still on his eye. The other three nodded.

"She couldn't have been in this town for more than an hour, and you say she did something to deserve a fight with four grown men?" Gabe was puzzled by their response.

"She broke the windshield on Jason's truck." Jeff pointed to his brother, though the words were a bit slurred because of his fat lower lip.

"And she stole all of Jeff's CDs, then threw them all one by one in the ditches all around town. We *still* haven't found them all," Joe added.

"She filled Josh's locker with beer and got him expelled! Twice! And she got him kicked off the football team. We needed him for the state championship!" Jason was practically yelling at this point.

Until that last statement, Gabe wondered why he had let the woman go. She had committed more crimes in one hour than the town had seen in months. "Guys, I assume that was a long time ago. I don't think it was worth a bar fight, was it?"

They all looked at the tabletop and shook their heads. Though she didn't win the fight, the boys had little fight left in them. Which would make the rest of his shift nice and easy.

"I should arrest all four of you for that fight." Gabe told them.

Jason looked up. "You should arrest her. She started it!"

"I might arrest you all. Then I can tell the paper to write a story about you boys getting licked by a girl who is barely five feet tall and a hundred pounds soaking wet. And I'll make sure that the reporter gets in there that Joey had his balls kicked so hard he now sings soprano."

The four started to mutter about not needing to arrest anyone. Satisfied, Gabe turned and walked away, suppressing a smile. No wonder she knew all the cops in this town. If she had done all those things to one family, what else had she been up to back then?

Gabe paid for his supper as he tried to remember the mother he had supposedly run off with. He had never run off with anyone, much less anyone in this town. He had barely been in this town since joining the Marines. His parents had been new to the area when he had enlisted, and he hadn't come back often enough to remember anyone. Grabbing his change, he looked at the bartender and asked, "Dave, do you want to press charges on anyone for the fight tonight?"

Dave looked over at the corner the fight had taken place in. Even he knew it was best to not make waves. "Nope."

Gabe sighed and nodded. "Do you have a bill for the soldier in the fight?"

"For Zoey? No, the burger was on the house. She always eats free when I'm working." Picking up a cloth, Dave cleaned the counter. The bartender knew almost everyone around. It was no surprise he knew the redhead since she was from the area.

"For serving our country?" Gabe lifted her hat, reminding him of her service.

"Nope, but I guess she did that, too. She gets to eat free for telling the cops she rolled my truck on Christmas Eve night during our senior year. I would've missed going on the senior ski trip if I had gotten into trouble one more time. She took the heat, and I owe her big time. It was during that trip that I finally got Kelly to notice me, and we've been together ever since. Oh, and Zoey let me cheat off her in algebra. I probably wouldn't have graduated without her help, so yeah, I owe her a lot." Dave grabbed Gabe's dirty plate and cleaned under them.

Gabe nodded, starting to see that she wasn't the troublemaker she seemed to be. "You must know who Zoey Connor Hart's parents are, then? I need to bring her this hat; she dropped it during the fight." He added the excuse about the hat since he was mainly asking for the name of her parents.

"Zoey Connor Hart?" The bartender asked, puzzled. He picked up a rag and began cleaning the counter in front of him while looking at the hat. "It's just Hart. Charley and Connie Hart were her parents. They're both gone, though. Her sister is Evie Singleton. She's the sexy one at the farmer's market. She lives about seven miles north of town, off number eleven."

Overhearing the conversation, the guy at the end of the bar added, "Connie was actually Catherine Connor. Her dad owned the Bank for a while, so Connor is probably from that. I went to school with her, and she was a redhead, too."

Gabe thanked them both for the information and headed out. He still had no idea who her parents were, but apparently, he and the mother were linked somehow.

Gabe looked at his watch. He would have to stop at the nursing home and talk to his mother some time to see if she knew anything about this woman. His mom didn't remember much that happened recently, but her memory was spot on for anything that happened a long time ago. Especially if it was back when they were new to town. She loved small town gossip.

Once Gabe got back in his cruiser, he threw the hat on the dash and looked at it for a moment, wondering more about Zoey. Everything he learned about her only seemed to make her more interesting. The hat made his car smell faintly of apples, recalling the feeling of her in his arms again. Pushing those feelings away, she was definitely too young for him. It didn't matter that she acted interested in him; he shouldn't be interested in her. Not at all.

Gabe started up the cruiser and continued his week-long shift of night patrol by heading north on eleven. It was his duty to make sure Zoey made it home after the fight without running into any car trouble. And he had her hat—she would need that, wouldn't she?

CHAPTER 4

THE SISTERS HAD SPENT HALF the night talking, and Zoey spent the other half staring at the ceiling, trying to sleep. Every time her eyes closed, sights and sounds from across the world came flooding back.

At four, she gave up any hope of sleep for that night. With a growl, she finally got out of bed. Padding over to her dresser, she felt around in the dark for something that she could run in. Coming up with a sports bra and shorts, she threw them on in the dark—she was going for a run.

Running had always cleared her mind, and today was no different as she ran down the gravel roads of her youth. Stopping to get her bearings just as the sun began to peek over the trees, she looked around. From her vantage spot, she could see for miles in every direction thanks to the flat terrain and the fact that there were no crops yet planted in the fields around her. To her in the dark, it hadn't changed at all in eight years, not the land at least. Daylight might change that, but until then she could surround herself in the familiarity of the past.

Zoey figured she was now about four miles from Evie's house. Everyone would be getting up soon, so it was probably a good idea to start heading back; she didn't want to run into anyone yet.

Looking around the yard, she walked up the driveway and was

glad to be back home. Even Evie seemed happy she had returned to Birch Cove. Zoey hoped she was just as happy that she wanted to stay.

Since their dad had died, Evie had been doing most of the farming alone, though she had their neighbor helping sometimes and had been hiring a neighbor kid for a few years. But Zoey knew the farm was more than one person could handle. Even her capable sister.

Evie had changed their dad's grain farm into a vegetable farm with some animals and some small grains, exactly what she'd always wanted. Even when Zoey had been in high school, she and Evie had spent Friday evenings selling veggies, canned goods, and homemade stuff at the farmer's market.

In the cool dark, she could still feel the scorching sun beating down on them as the town bought the tomatoes they worked all summer to grow. But now things were a little different around here. From Evie and Della's calls and letters, she knew they were now selling at a market in the Twin Cities, in addition to the one in Birch Cove. Meat had been added in the form of chickens and pigs, and the gardens had grown by leaps and bounds.

Della had once mentioned that Evie had been offered a booth at another farmer's market but had to turn it down because she was stretched too thin. Della had also said she wasn't going to be able to help as much anymore, now that she was trying to make partner at her law firm in Minneapolis.

That's why, when Zoey was offered an honorable discharge two weeks ago, she took it. She needed out. The Army had taken a lot out of her, and she was drained. She needed to get back to her family. She just hoped they needed her just as much.

Remembering the blue-eyed officer from the bar, she wondered how long he had been in the military and if he had problems sleeping as well. Did his hair get messed up when he was sleeping? She tried to get the image of him in bed out of her head. He probably looked pretty good outside of his polyester uniform—he certainly had felt good under it.

"Stop," she said out loud, picking up her pace the rest of the way back to Evie's, running from the images playing in her head. Like always.

CHAPTER 5

Gabe made it back to the station just as the sun came up to fill out paperwork before his shift ended. Walking into the station, he saw the day shift getting ready for their briefing. His buddy Allen Parker smiled and handed him a coffee as Gabe sat down at his desk. "I hear you tangled with Zoey Hart last night." Parker was grinning from ear-to-ear as if he had just told one hell of a joke. Allen had been at the Birch Cove department his entire career and was around the same age as Gabe. Allen *had* to have known about Zoey's wild days.

"Yup, a bar fight with the Jensen boys," Gabe said matter-of-factly, hoping Allen would let the topic drop.

"I heard you had to drag her out after she put two on the ground. She was getting ready to smoke 'em all, and you had to go and bust it up." Allen slapped him on the back in excitement over what he had heard about the evening.

Raising an eyebrow, Gabe asked his friend, "Should I not have broken it up, Parker?"

Allen sat down on the side of Gabe's desk and sighed. "I guess you needed to break it up, but those boys have needed the you-know-what kicked out of them for years now, and Zoey should be the one to do it. Hey, Don," Allen called out across the room with a laugh. "Do you remember when Zoey Hart broke Jeff's Jensen's windshield at the spring dance?"

"It was Jason's," Gabe mumbled.

Allen looked at him oddly. "No, it was Jeff's. She broke Jason's at graduation with a pellet gun. She broke all his windows—every one of 'em." Then he yelled a little louder, "Don, weren't you the one who had to fish her out of Roy Anderson's pond just to arrest her? She didn't think you'd go in after her, but you did anyway."

"Yeah, that was me. I still hate the water; she tried to drown me that day. Twice!" Don Young yelled back, holding up two fingers to prove the point. Gabe didn't look over at Young, but he could tell he was smiling.

"Is she back for good? We'll need more staff if she is. Her rap sheet would be miles long if she hadn't been a minor when most of that stuff happened. Did the military straighten her out? I guess not if she's back and fighting with the Jensen boys. Chief Martin was wrong about the military being good for her. I haven't seen her since her dad passed, and that was years ago... Maybe five." Gabe took another sip of coffee and glanced up at Allen, who was smiling fondly as he reminisced with Young. He had known Allen long enough to know that he liked the Zoey that got in so much trouble. It seemed like they all did.

"I don't know if she's back; she didn't say either way. She was in her uniform, though." Gabe failed to mention that she was a 'former corporal,' and that he didn't give her the opportunity to talk about her future plans—he was too busy just holding her in his arms.

"Come on, Don, we'd better go make sure the high school isn't on fire again with Zoey's back in town." With that, Allen jumped up to start his workday before Gabe could ask if Zoey had actually started a fire at the school before.

Ignoring the surrounding conversations, he worked for another half an hour until the room grew quiet as everyone headed out. Gabe looked around to see if anyone was still there, and when he saw the room was basically empty, he quickly downed the rest of his coffee and searched the station's database for Zoey Hart. Immediately, he found the file he was looking for and saw that her middle name was Connor. How had she gotten her middle name listed as her official name? She was twenty-nine, and her birthday was coming up. The file said she was five-foot-five, but he knew that she couldn't reach that height without a good-sized box under her feet. The weight listed was double what she was today—was it a misprint?

From the stories he'd heard tonight, he knew she had been arrested many times, but the file was completely empty, totally blank. Why was there even a file if it was empty? Where were all the arrests or even the warnings he had been told about? But the file was completely clean… Too clean. There was nothing but an old mug shot where she looked to be no more than twelve, but even in the mug shot, she had that mischievous smirk on her lips.

"You're not going to find anything on Zoey Hart, Watson. Chief Martin wiped it all when she joined the Army. It was their agreement." Allen had snuck up behind him when he was looking at the file. "She must be as hot as her sister if you're giving her another look. But she's a little young for you, and half the department is a little overprotective of her. Not saying that she would not be crazy between the sheets with all that red hair. You know how crazy redheads are." Putting his hat on, Allen laughed as he walked out the door.

Gabe turned off his computer and stared at the blank screen, tapping a pencil on his desk in frustration. He knew Allen was right—she was almost eleven years younger than him. Just a kid. But he couldn't get the image of her firm little body pressed against his out of his mind. Even her breasts had felt perfect against his chest, and he wished he had been able to touch them. And now, thanks to Allen, the image of her apple-smelling curls between his sheets would be stuck in his mind as well.

CHAPTER 6

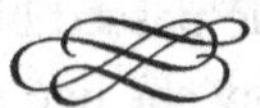

ZOEY WALKED into Evie's kitchen after her run to find both her sister and nephew were already up and eating breakfast. "Oh, you went for a run this morning," Evie stated, as she looked at Zoey's tennis shoes.

"Yeah, I needed to clear my head." *And it didn't work,* she thought, but didn't add. Zoey glanced at her nephew Ben, who was looking more like his mom every day. Both of them had green eyes and blond hair, though Ben's was cut short, and Evie's was in a long braid down her back. She looked the same as she had most of her adult life, except she had lost the bangs she used to have somewhere along the way. Both were dressed for the day in jeans and t-shirts, making Zoey feel underdressed in her sports bra and shorts.

"Morning, Zoey," Ben said when he saw her. At only eleven, Ben was already almost as tall as Zoey was. He was definitely going to take after his dad in that regard, but as far as Zoey could tell, that was the only trait Ben had picked up from Greg Singleton. Even now, years later, she still hated him as much as she had back then. But she loved his son with all her heart.

Zoey smiled at him. "Morning, Benny."

"Did you hurt your hand when you hit him?" No pleasantries from her nephew this morning, apparently.

"Who?" Zoey hoped the Jensen fight hadn't gotten around, but it looked like that cat was out of the bag.

"One of the Jensen boys. Clem called me and said you broke one of their noses," Ben said in wonder. Clementine Reed lived across the road with her grandparents and was Ben's age. They were the best of friends.

"Ben, leave Zoey alone. She maybe doesn't want to talk about it." Getting up from the table, Evie passed by her little sister. She touched Zoey on the head, the same way she had since they were young.

"I don't think anything's broken," Zoey feigned concern as she poured a cup of coffee. "Well, maybe his nose, but it had been broken before. And I used my head, so my hand doesn't hurt, see?" Zoey flexed her fingers to show her nephew nothing was wrong with it.

"Wow." Ben's eyes got bigger. "Can you show me how to fight?"

Evie slammed her coffee cup down on the counter, spilling some as she did it. "No, she cannot. You don't need to know how to fight, and Zoey doesn't need to fight anymore, either."

"That's right, Benny. No fighting is needed in Birch Cove. That's for Afghanistan." She didn't want her nephew to get in trouble by his mother on her account, but if he asked again, she would show him some moves. She remembered how tough it was to be a middle schooler.

As if on cue, a familiar horn from her part sounded, the bus. Both mother and son jumped up, and the young boy grabbed his backpack, scrambling out the door. When the bus finally pulled away, leaving the sisters alone, Evie asked, "Did you really have to get into a fight on your first day back?"

Zoey bristled. "It wasn't me. It was the Jensen's—they started it. I was just ending it, that's all. And no, I wasn't arrested."

Evie's green eyes bore into her. "That's not what I heard. I heard you were carried out by a cop. Dragged out, kicking and screaming."

The memory of Gabe Watson's hard back as she pounded her fists into it came rushing back to her, as did the feel of her world going straight for the first time in months, making her stop fighting him. But she wasn't going to think about that now.

"Well, yeah, I was. But he didn't arrest me. No warning even."

Zoey thought about the way his body felt as she slid down it. She felt her cheeks flushing a little at the memory.

"Which cop let you off? I heard you even threw a punch at him." Evie started loading the dishwasher, not noticing Zoey's red face.

"He blocked it. I think his name was Officer Watson." Zoey mumbled, hoping her sister did not catch the name clearly.

"The one mom ran off with? I heard he was back in town." Evie slammed the dishwasher closed and sat back down at the kitchen table.

"I think so, but I wasn't trying to get in trouble." She sounded like a kid again, trying to explain away her mistakes. But then again, she *was* making mistakes like a kid again. She had to prove she had grown up if she thought Evie would let her stay here and farm with her.

"It's time to stop getting into trouble, Zoey. I don't know what your plans are, but as long as you are here, but you have to stay out of that mess." Disappointment was heavily laced throughout her words. "I don't have time to constantly get you out of jail, okay?"

Zoey sat down as well and looked at the coffee cup in her hands. After a moment, she looked her older sister in the eyes and said, "I did not come back here to be the same 'me' that left. I came back to be like you. I want to work the land and help you so that we can make this Farmers Market thing even better than you're doing with it now. I want to help you expand also. Do the things you never had time for. And I have some ideas that might help."

"Well then," Evie squeezed Zoey's hands and smiled. "We have a lot to do, including getting Dad's house ready for you. I mean, if you want it. Nobody has lived there since he died, so it needs some work to just get it livable. It's still full of his stuff."

"You never went through his stuff?" Zoey asked in disbelief. It had been five years!

"No, I didn't want to do it alone, so I waited until one of my sisters came home and could help. And here you are," Evie laughed. "Get a shirt on so we can get started on your first day of farming. Maybe some pants, too."

Zoey looked down at the sports bra and shorts she had thrown on hours ago for her run, laughing at her sister's joke. They had all done their fair share of farm work growing up. Zoey had done even more since she was always in trouble, and putting in more hours on the farm was the way their father had punished her. In fact, she probably still owed him some hours of labor from high school.

Zoey went up to the spare room she had been given yesterday. She hated disappointing Evie already, and was determined to not let it happen again. From now on, she had to stay out of trouble and away from Officer Hunk.

CHAPTER 7

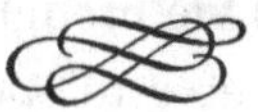

ROCK MUSIC WAS SLOWLY BLASTING AWAY the nightmare that had woken Zoey less than an hour ago, sending her out into the chilly night to once again clear her mind. As she ran, the moon was high in the sky, and the stars were twinkling away, but Zoey was still seeing the images that would not let her sleep. She'd been home for three days and had slept around an hour each night. Her body was exhausted, but her mind seemed to be working in overdrive.

She had put in three full days of physical labor on the farm. It was spring and most of the plants that were started in the greenhouses needed to be transferred to the gardens. All the little plants that were already in the garden needed to be weeded, and the baby chickens needed to be fed and watered at least twice a day. Zoey had no idea how Evie had done it on her own. It was taking them both all day just to finish everything that needed to be done.

They had taken a few hours off yesterday, but that was only to finally venture into their father's house. It had looked the same as when Zoey had lived there eight years ago, except for the layer of dust and the musky smell of an abandoned house. They filled garbage bags with clutter that their father hadn't been able to part with in life, only stopping when the back end of Evie's pickup was full. It had taken hours, but the house was still full and still smelled stale.

At least Zoey was able to retrieve some of her clothes from high school, so she would have more than one pair of jeans and a few t-shirts to wear. *The plus side of not sleeping and having lost most of her appetite was that she could easily fit in her high school jeans—worst diet ever!* She was happy that she wouldn't have to go shopping for more clothes this weekend when she and Evie brought back Della's car. There was no *way* she was going to be able to spend hours in a mall. Just the thought of having to keep her eye on all those people was making her nerves raw.

The song switched from a newer one she didn't know to one that had blasted from her car speakers the years she had sped down these gravel roads. A thousand memories flooded her mind as she kept up her running pace. She closed her eyes, trying to capture the nostalgic feelings coursing through her, wanting the feeling to last forever.

The song was entering the second verse when she opened her eyes, only to have a bright light shining at her. Leaving the middle of the road, she moved to the shoulder, expecting the car to pass her. Instead, the car slowed down and kept pace to her left. She glanced at it, noticing it was a cop car, or, more specifically, a cop SUV. Zoey pulled off her headphones as she slowed her pace, preparing to tell the officer she didn't need a ride.

"Need a lift?" Came the voice from the dark interior as the window lowered.

"No, thanks, I'm just out for a run. Thanks for asking," she replied as she jogged in place to prove she was just out for a run. Then she took off slowly so that the cop would know he could leave, but heard the SUV stop and a car door open. At the sound, she picked up speed, confident she could outrun any cop on the force in Birch Cove. She had been running every day for years while they drive around in cars.

Within a few steps, the cop grabbed her arm, pulling her to a stop instantly. Zoey's arm tingled where his hand was still touching her, and the panic she should've felt was oddly missing. She couldn't see his face with the car's headlights shining so brightly behind him, but she didn't need to. She knew it was Officer Watson; somehow, her body remembered his touch.

He growled, pulling her around to face him. "You can't go for a run at 2:30 in the morning, Red."

"Why? Is it against the law to run in this town?" Snapping back, she was suddenly angered by his tone and the use of a nickname she hated. She was well aware of her hair color.

"It is not against the law, but it *is* against your better judgment. You're running down the middle of a gravel road wearing nothing but black, and you're wearing headphones so you can't hear someone coming." He was still holding her arm when he grabbed the headphones out of her hand. "Do you want to be hit by a car?"

Looking down at her black shorts and black sports bra, she wasn't going to explain what she ran in. Now that she had stopped running, exhaustion was hitting her hard. She didn't even have the strength to fight him as he led her back to the patrol car. Still holding on to her arm, he opened the car's front passenger door. "Get in," he hissed, obviously angry at her. She had no strength to start a fight at this point, so she got in the car.

It smelled like him, some sort of masculine scent Zoey couldn't identify, but it was calming. *Get ready for the tongue lashing of your life, Zoey*, she thought as she watched him walk around the car to get to the driver's side. He took off his light jacket just before he slid into the driver's seat, and she watched him throw her headphones onto the dash next to a hat—her hat. She sat up straighter. "That's my hat. Where'd you find it?"

"Lobo's after you took off. I talked to the Jensen boys about the fight. It seems they have a lot of grievances against you." He was smiling as he added, "Something about a windshield, some stolen CDs, and a certain locker and beer incident."

Zoey narrowed her eyes a little. "They deserved it. They were such big bullies back then, and I had to defend practically everyone against them. They were the reason I got into trouble all the time." She knew her history with the Jensen boys was rocky, and that's why she was staying away from town. One of the reasons, at least.

* * *

THE JENSEN BOYS had not changed; they were still the bullies she used to battle years before. Gabe simply stared at her for a moment, taking her in again. It had been three days since the fight at the bar, and this was the first time he had seen or heard anything from her. When he came upon the lone runner in the middle of the gravel road, he instantly knew it was her. Just as instantly, he was angry with her for putting herself in danger.

As Gabe continued to look over at her, his anger dissipated at seeing the exhaustion in her eyes. He reached back to grab his jacket, then handed it to her. "Put this on, Zoey. You must be freezing. I'll take you home."

It was forty-nine degrees out, and though she had been running, she was wearing next to nothing. In fact, he was having a hard time keeping his eyes on her face instead of taking in every exposed inch of her body. She was amazingly put together.

"I'm not cold, and I can get home on my own. You interrupted my run." Even though she said the words, she pulled the jacket around her like a blanket and snuggled into the heated seat he had turned on for her a second ago.

"How far did you make it this time?" He tried to hide a smile as he put the car into gear.

"Four miles," she mumbled, her eyes already starting to droop.

"Then why are you seven miles from your sister's house?" The anger threatened to surface again—she was running blindly through the night! It was only a matter of time before a car hit her. "How long has it been since you last slept?"

She turned to look at him through her half-closed eyes. He couldn't tell if she was almost asleep or scowling at him. Maybe a little of both. "Weeks." her words were so quiet he barely heard her.

"Do you want to talk about it? I was over there, too." He reached out and took her hand in his, giving it a gentle squeeze. She needed to talk. Being in a war zone is hard on the body and the mind, but it's sometimes just as hard when you leave that war zone behind. Just letting down your guard and not being on high alert takes time, sometimes a lot more than the experts think. It's hard to turn that off.

Gabe wondered if she was dodging the question, but then heard her deep, steady breathing. She had fallen asleep with her hand still in his, but now her grip was tighter than a moment ago. She was holding on to him as if her life depended on it. Looking down at their joined hands and then back to her relaxed, sleeping face, Gabe felt a surge of emotions. The need to protect her was overwhelming.

Stopping on the shoulder of the gravel road, he pulled his hand away from hers, trying not to wake her, then eased her head and body from its awkward position to the center console. He had done it so that she would not get a kink in her neck, but the move had also put those stunning red curls close enough that Gabe could touch them. Taking her small, warm hand in his again, he hoped it made her feel safe. In a small way, he was trying to protect her.

He awkwardly put the car into gear with his left hand and slowly drove the seven miles to her sister's house. The smell of fresh apples soon filled the car, and when he got there, he didn't have the heart to wake her from the sleep she so desperately needed. After just a moment of hesitation, he drove past the dark house, letting Zoey sleep.

CHAPTER 8

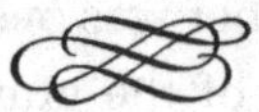

ZOEY SLOWLY BECAME aware she had fallen asleep in a car. Cracking an eye open, she realized it wasn't just any car. Her head was resting on the center console, and her body was curled into a ball on the passenger seat of Gabe Watson's cruiser.

Which would get her sent packing by Evie faster? Being brought home by a cop or *this* cop? With a start, she noticed he was holding her hand...or was she holding his? She quickly let go and bolted upright.

"You can't take me home.," she blurted out, instantly hearing the panic in her voice and wanting to take it back.

"Zoey, I have to take you home." Gabe was stretching the numbness out of his newly released arm and hand.

She glanced at the clock on the car dash. It was just after five in the morning. "No, you don't understand. I can't be taken home in a cop car; Evie will think I got in trouble. She'll never believe I'm not... Wait, am I in trouble?" Her head was spinning about. What all happened in the last almost three hours since she was picked up? She couldn't remember anything.

"No, you're not in trouble, though I think you should rethink your exercise time. Maybe more in the daytime and less after midnight,"

Gabe said before adding, "What would your sister do if I brought you home right now?"

Looking over at him, she could see enough of his face in the dashboard lights to know he was joking with her, but she certainly didn't see it as a joke. "I don't know. Kick me out for being too much trouble? I haven't been here very long, and she has a lot on her plate right now. She doesn't need me screwing up all the time and making a mess of things."

"But you aren't in trouble," he reminded her.

"I would be if *you* brought me home. You're not welcome on Hart land." She knew it was true. Having been raised by a heartbroken man after Gabe stole his wife, she knew her sister would definitely not be pleased to see him.

"What did I do?" He calmly asked, but there was an anger brewing behind those clear blue eyes. "Oh, wait. I stole your mother. Except I didn't. I don't even know your mother."

Why did he have to bring it up when the night had been so nice? Well, sleeping had been nice, but maybe he didn't enjoy it as much as she had. As Evie's house came into view, Zoey blurted out, "Stop the car. I'll get out here."

"No," he shook his head and kept driving. "You have to believe me. I have no idea who your mother is."

"From what I heard, you had come home after completing basic training to visit your parents, and when you left, you left with a woman named Connie. That doesn't ring a bell? You don't even remember her?" Zoey couldn't believe it. She had spent years wondering if they were happy together, and he couldn't even remember her.

"Dave at the bar said your mom's name was Catherine. Not Connie," Gabe said as he stopped the car on the side of the road, less than a mile from Evie's house.

"Catherine Connor Hart, but she went by Connie most of her life to honor her family who built most of Birch Cove." Zoey couldn't remember what all they owned through the years, but the bank and a sawmill were two of the businesses. In fact, her grandparents on her mother's side had lived in an old mansion on Maple Street that had been in the family for generations. Zoey's mom had a hard time excepting life as a farmer's wife and had put up with it for just over fifteen years before bailing on her poor husband and three daughters. Zoey hadn't seen her since that day. It was beginning to sound like Gabe hadn't, either.

"I took a woman to the bus station in Minneapolis that day, but I don't remember her name. I don't remember much about that day, to be honest. I had a lot going on, and I was heading to Iraq soon. It was only a few hours and I barely remember her. Though she had red hair like you, though, maybe not nearly as curly." As he talked about her hair, he reached out and gently grabbed a curl by her cheek, pulling it straight, then letting it go and watching it bounce back into a curl.

She watched the clear blue of his eyes go stormy as he played with her hair. She couldn't remember anyone touching her hair with such fascination. His fingers found the curl again and tucked it into place, and her breath caught as his fingers slowly slid over the back of her ear while his thumb traced over the front of it. She watched his eyes in fascination as that stubborn curl fell from behind her ear and landed back on her cheek.

Her heart raced as his hand traveled slowly down her ear to the back of her neck. A quiet moan escaped her lips as Gabe pulled her head to meet his in the middle of the car. Letting him guide her willingly, maybe eagerly, until his lips touched her cheek at the spot the wayward curl was resting against. She didn't dare breathe in case it made him stop, closing her eyes instead as a sudden heat bloomed throughout her body.

With one hand still sliding down her spine, his other hand reached up and guided her chin to meet his mouth. His warm lips were like a butterfly's wings against hers, but soon became heavier. She parted her lips as Gabe's mouth touched hers for a third time, urging him to deepen his kiss. Then the damn radio between them came to life, causing Zoey to nearly jump out of her skin.

Gabe groaned in frustration as his hands and arms all pulled away from her, leaving her feeling cold as he reached for the radio to answer the call. She didn't hear what was coming through the radio or what he was saying into it—her mind was focused on how to get out of his cruiser.

Shrugging out of the jacket, she swung open the door. He didn't say anything, but she knew he wouldn't as long as he was on the police radio. Slamming the door shut, she took off at a sprint for Evie's house. She could already see lights on in the house from where she was, which meant that Evie was already up.

She had just managed to turn down the driveway when she saw Gabe's car drive slowly past her on the gravel road. He was determined to make sure she got home safely. Stopping in the drive, she watched in disbelief until his taillights disappeared down the road.

When they were gone, she was able to start towards the house, this time at a walk. She needed time to get over what had happened in Gabe's car before she saw her sister. What *had* happened? Had she really let him kiss her after he told her he couldn't even remember her mother? Had she given in so easily? What would've happened if the radio hadn't interrupted them?

Cheeks still red with embarrassment as she entered the house, Zoey hoped her sister would think it was from the chilly morning run. Putting a hand on her wildly beating heart to try to control her erratic heart rate, she was happy to see Evie and Ben were not in the kitchen yet. With relief, she ran up to her bedroom and grabbed a pile of clothes for the day, taking them into the bathroom. Successfully avoiding her sister for now.

But the hot shower was no escape, as her mind wouldn't stop thinking about Gabe's soft lips on her cheek and mouth. Her spine tingled where he had run his hand down it. His touch had been so light, so warm. Would he have kept going? Would he have dragged her over the center console so that she was on top of him? Would she have stopped him? Ever?

Knowing the answer, she hated herself for it. She hated how this man made her feel safe and sexy at the same time, and she hated how much she wanted him. She turned off the hot water in hopes a cold shower would stop her from thinking about Gabe, but knew it wouldn't help.

When she finally entered the kitchen, she was ready to face her sister. Ben was absent this morning, leaving the sisters alone. Maybe Zoey wasn't as ready as she had thought she was without the buffer of her nephew.

"How was your run?" Evie was pouring herself a steaming cup of coffee as she spoke.

"Good." Zoey didn't go into it any deeper.

"You shouldn't get up so early to run. If you want to run, you can do it during the day. Maybe I've been working you too hard these last few days." Evie sat down with a coffee cup in her hands. "You look a bit more rested today, though. Did you finally get some sleep?"

Zoey almost dropped the cup she had been taking out of the cabinet. Evie knew she wasn't sleeping. How? She grabbed the cup to her chest, glad it didn't break. "No, that's okay. I like to run early before my day starts, and I was able to catch a few hours last night."

"I don't like you running in the dark." Evie crossed her arms as she spoke. "Were you wearing the same thing you had on yesterday? You're going to get hit by a car, you know."

"I'm used to running in the dark." Zoey defended herself. She didn't confirm what she wore to her sister because Evie had enough material for this lecture. Gabe had also brought them up. It's not like she had a wardrobe to pick from; she had enough clothes for a single drawer right now. The rest of her dresser was empty.

"Well, at least wear clothes that reflect light." Evie stared at her from over her coffee cup for a moment before mercifully changing the subject. "Also, we're going to bring Della back her car today. We can go to the mall and get you something more appropriate to wear if you insist on running in the dark. And some more work clothes, too. You can't be washing clothes every other day, and all those jeans you brought home yesterday have holes in them."

"I can't do the mall," Zoey mumbled as Ben walked into the kitchen with his pajamas still on.

Evie looked at her baby sister and sighed. "Maybe Della has some clothes you can use then. She might be willing to part with some shirts and pants, and she's way closer to your size, shorty."

Zoey smiled at her big sister's old nickname for her. Evie was right.

Della and Zoey were basically the same size, while Evie was a few inches taller than them. "Yeah, that would be better."

"Sounds like a plan. One of us has to go over to your place and feed the chickens and pigs before we go," Evie announced, finishing the last of her coffee.

"I'll go feed the pigs so you can feed this one." Zoey pointed to her nephew and headed out the door without touching the coffee she had poured for herself.

As she passed her big sister, Evie snagged her into a bear hug. "I miss you, Zoey," she whispered before letting go. Zoey walked out the door, wondering why her sister used 'miss' instead of 'missed.' Could Evie sense that Zoey's mind was off somewhere else?

Getting into Evie's truck, she realized she had left her phone in Gabe's cop car. *Great*, she thought. *When am I going to get that back?* How was she going to explain that one to her sister? It was just a short drive to her future farm, where she fed and watered both the baby chicks that lived in the barn and the dozen or so pigs. She enjoyed the daily trips to her house to take care of the animals there; it was also an excuse to survey her land. Her dreams were finally coming true.

Zoey was happy to have finally gotten some sleep last night, even if it was in Gabe's car. Her head was clearer than it had been in months, and she was excited to spend the day with her sister. When she had flown into Minneapolis, Della couldn't get away from work to pick her up but had told Zoey to take a taxi to her apartment and take the car. That's what Zoey had done, and then she had headed back to Birch Cove with only two stops before Evie's house. One to get her long hair cut off, and the second to get a Lobo Burger. One had gone well, and the other had left her wanting to spend more time with a certain cop.

She let herself remember holding his hand and feeling safe, as if the world wasn't closing in on her. Maybe tonight she would sleep on her own, since the nightmares were kept at bay for now. Maybe she could get more than three hours of sleep in her own bed, all soft and secure. But in her heart, she was worried that she had only slept so well because Gabe was there, holding her hand... Keeping her safe.

CHAPTER 9

THE TWO-HOUR DRIVE to Minneapolis in Della's car had been uneventful, especially since Evie couldn't call to berate Zoey for losing her cell phone. That was a fight best not relived. Zoey parked her sister's gray car in the same spot she had found it days before, and as she watched Evie pull her big truck into the spot behind her, Zoey was surprised at how long it felt since she was at Della's apartment. At least she was feeling a lot better and was more comfortable back on the land where she wanted to be.

Evie and Ben jumped out of the cab after it parked, and all three of them walked up to the three-story apartment building that was her oldest sister's home. Before they made it to the door, it burst open, and Della rushed out to hug Zoey as tight as Evie had a few days before.

"You look skinny," Della whispered to her baby sister.

"You look weird," Zoey laughed. Her sister's red curls were now a mousy brown straight bob. Della had always shared the burden of red curls. Zoey thought the color made her sister look older than her thirty-two years, but maybe that's what she was going for.

"Shut up and come in." Della laughed but didn't let go of Zoey completely as they walked up the two flights of stairs to her apartment. Once there, Della finally let her go, and Zoey noticed that the place was smaller than she thought it would be. In her mind, Della was a powerful lawyer who should've lived in a large apartment, but what she had was a one-bedroom, tiny little place. Ben was already in the living room with the TV on, flipping through the channels, so Zoey took a stool at the counter next to Evie.

"Nice place," Zoey managed, even though the place didn't even look lived in.

"Thanks, but I don't spend a lot of time here. When you have to put in over eighty hours in the office, you don't spend a lot of time at home." Della poured coffee for the three of them.

Zoey was astonished as she wrapped her hands around the hot cup in front of her. Della had been at the same firm for ten years. "Why do you have to put in so many hours?"

Evie cut in with the answer. "So she can make partner and put in even *more* hours. It's all part of the plan, Zoey." Evie's tone made it perfectly clear what she thought of the plan. Della may have been the oldest, but Evie was the mama hen to them both.

"The plan?" Zoey hadn't heard anything about this before, but she hadn't been around either.

"Evie doesn't like the plan, but I do plan to be a partner at this firm by thirty-five, and then a judge by forty-five. A *judge*, Evie." Della was looking at Zoey when she replied, but aimed the last comment at her other sister.

Zoey had no doubt that the plan had been hatched early in Della's life—she had always been the smart one. Their parents had enrolled her in school a year early, and she had managed to skip a few more grades before she graduated from high school. So, even though she and Evie were only nineteen months apart in age, Della had graduated five years before her younger sister. It seemed to Zoey that Della had always had her life figured out.

Zoey looked between her sisters, who couldn't have been more different in personality, not to mention in looks as well, with Della's short dark hair and Evie's long blond braid. But if you took that away and looked at their features, they looked so much alike. Zoey tried to cut the tension. "Okay, enough with the plan talk. We all have plans."

"Do you have plans, Zoey?" Della asked

"I have an incredibly messy house to get in order, and I have to learn everything Evie can teach me about farming. Basically, I just need to get my life going," Zoey sighed. It didn't sound like a lot, but it sure felt like it.

"But first, she needs clothes," Evie bumped her shoulder with Zoey's.

"Let's go shopping then!" Della got excited—she was a complete shopaholic and had been for years. She may not spend a lot on housing, but she could certainly spend a lot on other stuff.

Zoey glanced at Evie, hoping for some help from her sister. Evie winked and grabbed her older sister around the waist. "No, Dell, we're shopping in your closet today. She doesn't feel like going to the mall right now, so I brought her to raid your closet. She's too small for my clothes, but you guys are basically the same size."

"Well then, let's go look." Della and Evie exchanged a look, but she didn't question her sisters after that. She just led them into her tiny bedroom and threw open the closet doors.

Zoey looked at the walk-in closet that was stuffed full of clothing, from work suits to jeans. It was like going to a clothing store, but everything would fit her. She couldn't stop the tears from welling up in her eyes—her sisters were saving her. From giving her a place to stay to giving her clothes without making her do things she wasn't ready for. She looked around the closet, getting her emotions under control. Grabbing a few sweatshirts and jeans, she folding them over her arm one by one.

Walking out of the closet with an arm full and her emotions under control, she threw the pile on the bed. Looking at the clothes, Evie started to fold them and put them into piles, and as she did, she said, "She needs workout clothes, too. She runs around in only these little shorts and a sports bra. They're both black, and she's running in pitch darkness."

"Evie, no." Zoey didn't need to have both sisters harping on her about running. It was her only escape right now, and she needed that escape.

"I have what she needs." Della turned to her dresser. "You shouldn't run at night, though. It's dangerous. Evie, let her run during the daytime—you can't work her all day, so she has to exercise in the dark." Della's words made it sound like it was Evie's fault, not Zoey's.

"I'm *not* making her run at night. I'd let her run whenever she wants, but she never asks," Evie shot back.

Della had opened a drawer in her dresser and started pulling out wads of spandex. "Here, I got these when I started exercising last year, but then work got in the way, so I quit. You can have almost all of them, but I'll keep an outfit or two in case I get a little time and can do it again. But I don't need all of these."

Della looked up after piling an entire drawer full into Zoey's arms. Zoey was simply smiling at her. "What?" Della asked, confused.

"Your red hair's coming out. All these wild prints and crazy designs? Nobody with that mousy hair would buy all this. Only a redhead," Zoey laughed, then she laughed a little more because the outfits were exactly what she would have picked out herself.

"I don't have red hair." Della touched her straight dark tresses. "I spend a lot of money to not have red, curly hair."

"You should spend less and embrace it. Sister, you have red hair," Evie stated from the bed, throwing a shirt at Della's head.

Zoey dumped the exercise clothes in another pile on the bed since Evie was still folding the first. She was venturing back into the closet when she heard Evie add, "Just like Zoey, look at those curls. They're so cute." Zoey smiled and remembered Gabe touching her hair, trying to control it…as well as the kisses that had followed. Heat rushed to her cheeks, and she had to stay in the closet longer to get her body temperature to return to normal.

"When did you cut off your hair, Zoey? Recently, I assume," Della called into the closet after her.

"Before I left Minneapolis the other day. I was tired of the hassle of long hair, and since the Army had no more say in my hairstyle, off it went." She walked out of the closet. She had had long hair for as long as she could remember, and for the last few months, she had thought of nothing but cutting it off. So, the first chance she got, she had.

"I can't believe how curly it is. Do you think mine would be like that?" Della touched her straightened hair again. They had the same color and waves when they were younger.

"I bet you would," Evie grinned, then added, "What would it take to get that straightening stuff out of it?"

Della backed away and put her hands up. "No way. I have worked at the image I want at the office. Nobody wants a crazy redhead with curls representing their company in court."

"Of course, they would," Zoey looked at her sister in confusion, "as long as you can *win*."

"I still think you should come back to Birch Cove and do family court. There are so many women who can't get a good lawyer in that town, and you could work out of the Connor Mansion. It would be perfect!" Evie gave Della a pleading look. The Connor Mansion was their maternal grandparent's house in Birch Cove, an old, gigantic house just off Main Street. The girls had inherited it from their grandparents, but nobody had lived in it for many years now.

"I like being a corporate lawyer," Della said, then sighed as she asked, "Who needs a good lawyer this time?"

Evie perked up at the question. "Beth Matthews, Katie Vaughn, Laura Jensen… To name three off the top of my head."

"Laura Anderson actually married *Jason Jensen*?" Zoey asked, eyes wide. Laura had been one of her good friends in high school, though she had not heard from her in years. Back then, Laura followed Jason around like a puppy, no matter what Zoey told her about him.

"Yes," Evie said. "And man, he has a mean streak in him."

"Why would she marry him then? Maybe it's a good thing I gave him a black eye," Zoey mumbled.

Della dropped another load of clothes on the bed. "Was this recently?"

Evie jumped in with a smile. "First day back. She got a haircut and then beat the daylights out of half the Jensen family. Only to be dragged away by a cop."

Zoey couldn't believe Evie was smiling and bragging about it. She had thought her sister was pissed about the fight, and now she was telling Della about it as if she'd been there. Rolling her eyes, Zoey went back into the closet in hopes they would stop talking about it. She didn't want to talk about her fight or how it was stopped. Or more to the point, by who.

Zoey grabbed another shirt, then walked out, changing the subject. "So, are either of you seeing anyone?" Both sisters stopped talking and started folding more intently, keeping their eyes on their work. "Nobody?" Zoey added with a grin.

Evie waved her off with the usual comeback. "Been there, done that. Not again."

"It's…complicated," Della quietly said into the pile of clothes she was folding.

Evie and Zoey both looked over at her. "What?" They asked in unison.

"It's complicated, okay? He works for the firm, so we can't really date. There are rules against that sort of thing," Della explained.

"Is he your boss?" Evie asked with interest.

"No, just a co-worker," Della looked back at Evie, her lips pressed into a thin line.

"Do you get to see him much, then?" Zoey wondered how a relationship like that would even work. Not that she was an expert on the subject, but even she saw the flaws in this one.

She nodded. "We actually work together quite a bit, so we actually get to spend a lot of time together. We just don't get to date much."

"Doesn't sound like quality time, sounds like work time," Zoey observed. She saw Evie nod in agreement as she picked up a shirt and began folding it.

"We spend time together. We just have to be creative about it," Della argued back.

"Do you drag him back here and have your wicked way with him, then? Or do you just make out in closets?" Zoey demanded, waggling her eyebrows at Della.

"No, and no!" Was Della's only response.

"You should bring him out to the farm one weekend so we can size him up," Evie cut in, smiling first at Zoey, then Della.

Della shook her head. "No, I don't think he'd like the farm too well. He's not much of a country boy or a getting dirty kind of boy. He's a man, not a boy."

Zoey walked over to her oldest sister and gave her a big hug, whispering, "Does he know that the curtains don't match the drapes?"

Evie looked at her in exasperation. "Zoey, really?"

"Really, *Evie*, we are three grown women. Can't we talk about sex?" Della asked, starting to fill bags with folded clothes.

"I-I just don't think we need to talk about it, okay?" Evie stuttered.

"To answer the question, in my experience, guys don't care much about it, Zoey. They don't seem to think too much once you get to that," Della explained with a wink.

"Nobody's ever said anything?" Zoey asked, amazed that Della would talk about sex so openly. Evie's cheeks were flame-red as she tried not to listen to the conversation.

"Nope, and I've been coloring my hair since college. No one's ever cared," Della said matter-of-factly.

"Have you slept with a lot of guys?" Zoey sat down on the bed and intently watched her oldest sister fold clothes. So much had happened in their lives that the other didn't know about.

"I've had my fair share. How about you, Zoey?" Della's green eyes bored into her.

"Not so many, I guess," Zoey admitted hesitantly. She really didn't want to get into it with her sisters.

"How about you, Evie? Have you had a lot of *lovers*?" Della turned to the sister, blushing on the bed. Possibly just to see her squirm some more.

"Della, I am not answering that." Evie covered her face with a sweatshirt.

"Maybe you need to get laid, Evie. You might not be so uptight." Della threw a pair of jeans on top of the sweatshirt Evie was hiding beneath.

Watching her sisters, Zoey felt happy for the first time in months. The situation brought back so many memories from their childhood— her two older sisters were always teasing and testing each other. Their personalities were so different, and they clashed over the littlest things. Though Evie was embarrassed, Zoey knew she could turn on a dime and have Della speechless. Both were over thirty, and they still acted like little kids at times, and she hoped they always would.

Biting her lip, Zoey tried not to cry over the years they had lost in each other's lives. Years wasted, barely talking. What would happen if they drifted apart again? What would happen if Evie sent her packing? Where would she go then? She had only one dream, and what would happen if that dream was gone?

"Della, you made her cry," Evie accused, as she nodded at Zoey.

Before Zoey could pull herself together, she felt arms around her. She couldn't tell who was hugging her because she couldn't see through the tears in her eyes. It didn't matter, though, because she felt a second pair of arms around her a moment later.

"We didn't mean to make you cry." Della was still holding Zoey.

"Della will stop talking about sex," Evie stated, more to Della than Zoey.

"It's not that; it's us." Zoey wiped her tears.

"Us?" Della leaned back to look at her little sister.

"This is one of the first times we have been together since Dad's funeral, and we really didn't spend much time together then."

"You're right. It's been years since we've actually just hung out together. Just that one vacation when you were in Florida, Zoey," Della agreed. That had been years before when Zoey had finished basic training.

"We can't let that happen again. We'll get together all the time now," Evie said, nodding.

"I'll come up more often, I swear," Della promised.

"I'm sorry I left and was gone for so long." Zoey looked from one sister to the other. She knew they spent most weekends at the farmer's market together.

Evie squeezed her again. "You were doing important things, Zoey. We know that."

"I should've never gone," Zoey whispered, wishing she had been here the entire time. She wished she hadn't been so much trouble that she had to be sent away.

"You didn't really have a choice," Della chuckled.

"I should've talked to you two before signing up." Looking back, she saw that maybe they could have helped, but at the time, she didn't think there was anything that could be done.

"You were a teenager, Zoey. They're not great communicators."

Evie nodded towards the living room where her soon-to-be-teenager was still watching TV.

"I wish you would have, too," Della said to Zoey.

"From now on, we talk about it. Whatever it is. Promise?" Evie smiled.

"Promise," Della agreed instantly.

"Promise," Zoey said with a laugh, but she knew she wasn't even close to ready to share what was going on in her life. What had happened was a secret that she didn't know if she would ever share—even with her sisters.

By the time Zoey and Evie had made it back to Birch Cove, it was getting close to dark. It had been a great day. Even though they hadn't left the apartment, they had had fun getting to know each other again, just getting to be sisters.

Della had ordered delivery, so they didn't have to go pick up dinner, and they sat and talked all day. Most of the time was spent talking about their dad and the past. Each of them carried baggage from those days, not just Zoey. Then they talked about the future and what the plans for the farm were. Evie didn't say much as Zoey and Della discussed plans for her house and the coming Farmer's Market season.

Zoey had let Ben sit in the front seat on the drive home, leaving mother and son to uphold most of the conversation. She just listened to them talk about what was happening in school and around the community, surprised by how many of the names she had never heard of.

Zoey decided that she would have to focus on getting her dad's house cleaned out and fixed up so she could move out of Evie's house. Evie and Ben didn't need her hanging around forever; they needed to get back to being a little family. And she desperately needed her own space.

Zoey had stopped paying attention to what was happening outside or wondering where they were on their journey home and was surprised when Evie stopped the truck in the driveway. "Ben, go get the mail." Her son jumped out of the truck.

When he climbed back in, he said, "Someone left their phone in our mailbox."

Zoey's eyes flew to her sister and then to her nephew, who was holding up her phone. "That's Zoey's phone. I wonder who found it?"

Sitting up so fast her seatbelt caught, she had to take it off to get her phone. Her headphones were neatly wrapped around the phone as well. "Was that all that was in there?" She asked her nephew, her heart pounding.

He smiled at her and said, "No, we got the newspaper, too."

Gabe still had her hat. Was it still sitting on his dash? She leaned back in the seat and looked at her cell phone? She had missed it today. There was one new message from an unknown number.

You need to set a lock on your phone. Hope you didn't get in trouble when you got home.

Smiling as she stared at the words, she couldn't even get mad about him possibly looking through her phone. She didn't really believe that he had gone through it, though; he was Gabe, after all. Somehow, she knew he wouldn't have invaded her privacy.

Evie pulled up to the house, and Zoey opened her door and grabbed the bags of clothes her sister had given her before going inside. Hopefully, she would be tired enough to get some sleep tonight.

CHAPTER 10

GABE DIDN'T KNOW how to feel just before three in the morning when he saw Zoey Connor Hart running along the side of the road in his headlights' glare again. He couldn't stop smiling long enough to be mad. He'd be lying to himself if he said he hadn't been driving around half the night looking for her, just to see if he was going to find her out running again tonight.

During this shift, he usually had a hard time sleeping. Getting good sleep in the middle of the day was nearly impossible for him, and today was no different. He had spent more time than he wanted to admit thinking about her when, really, he should've been getting the rest he needed. Unfortunately, the few hours he had been able to sleep were filled with her, too.

Pulling up alongside her, he rolled down the window and asked, "Do you need a ride?" At first, he thought she was going to ignore him on the long stretch of empty road, but she glanced at the cruiser and then smiled at him. He stopped the car, and to Gabe's amazement, she happily opened the door and slid into the passenger seat.

Plopping the earbuds from her ears as she reached behind her to put her seatbelt on, she mumbled, "Hi, thanks for stopping."

"I thought you weren't going to exercise in the middle of the night anymore?"

"But I'm wearing white, see? It reflects." She gestured at her tank top and shorts with a smirk.

Gabe looked also, instantly regretting it. The tank top was as tight-fitting as her sports bra was yesterday, only this time, Gabe could see that she wasn't wearing a bra beneath the thin white fabric. The outline of her perfect nipples beneath the tight fabric had his grip tightening on the steering wheel. *Don't even think about it, Gabe,* he thought to himself. *She's too young for you, and you know it.* Trying to look anywhere that wasn't going to cause him to drive off the road, he shifted his eyes to her shorts, and he saw that they, too, were tighter than her black ones. The entire outfit molded to her small frame as if it were tailored just for her, and he could've had it off her in three seconds flat.

Gabe shifted uncomfortably in his seat and started driving in hopes of getting his mind off her body in the white outfit. He swore he could see Zoey grinning at him in his peripheral. "I said, don't run at night."

"Actually," she argued, slowly running her hands down the front of her shirt, "you said don't run at night in *black*. This is white, and it fits really well. Completely different."

"Can we agree to disagree on this?" He gathered the willpower to pull his eyes forward again, desperately wanting to trail his hands down her body after hers. "Do you even know where you are?" He watched her stare out the dark window for a few minutes. When he thought she had decided not to answer the question, he pressed on, needing her to understand that what she was doing was dangerous, "Do you? How many miles have you ran?"

"It doesn't matter. I can find my way home once the sun comes up." Zoey shot him a smile and then winked.

"Were you really going to just run in a random direction for another three hours before you went home?" Gabe's anger was starting to win over his emotions now. "Evie's house is three miles southwest of here."

"Okay, now I know where I am. You can let me out now, thanks."

She put her headphones back in her ears as if she had just stopped him to ask for directions.

He reached over and grabbed her headphones' wire out of her hand, but dropped them on her lap as he said, "I'm taking you home."

Out of the corner of his eye, he saw her cross her arms and stare out the passenger window. She didn't turn away from the window when she asked in a near-whisper, "Can I just ride with you for a little while?"

His breath left him in a rush. "Yes." He knew he couldn't say no to her.

It took every ounce of strength he had to not stop the car and pull her into his arms. He wished he could protect her from everything in her head, from everything she was running from. What had happened that sent her out into the dark, night after night?

"Can I borrow your jacket again? It's a little chilly out tonight." As if to prove it, she shivered a little, and Gabe noticed the goosebumps on her arms and the tops of her tone thighs. After he had slipped the jacket off, he turned the heat up in the car.

"So, you couldn't sleep again? Do you want to talk about it? Talking about it does help. I went through it too, you know. After I came back and saw a psychiatrist for a while." He watched as she snuggled under his jacket like a blanket, tucking her legs under her so that that she was completely cocooned under the jacket.

"Nope," she answered from under her cover. "What works for some doesn't always work for everyone, and you were a Marine, which is very different from being in the Army." He could swear he heard her laughing at her own joke.

"Okay, we won't talk about the Army, then. How about that time you burned down the high school?" He was chuckling to himself when she sat up, and a look of panic flashed into her big brown eyes. Gabe's breath caught in his throat when the jacket fell to her waist, and he caught sight of her nipples straining through the white shirt again. He slammed his eyes back to the road ahead, clenching his jaw and forcing himself to breathe again.

"I didn't burn down the school." He felt her hand on his arm, the touch sending a sizzle of electricity throughout his lower body. "I swear it wasn't me. Everyone always blamed me for that, but I was only at the school because Leanna Harper had gotten some keys to the school, and we were getting the answers to a math test. Leanna chickened out, and I had to go alone. It had to have been bad wiring, and the fire only caused damage to that one classroom. It wasn't even the math one."

He could tell by how quickly she spoke that he had hit a nerve. I nerve that was still very raw. And maybe it was one of the reasons she wasn't going into town. But he knew it wasn't the only reason, and it wasn't why she was out tonight, not sleeping.

"My dad never believed I didn't do it, you know," she added, letting go of his arm and sitting back to stare out the windshield.

"He probably believed you before he died." Gabe put his hand over hers that was resting on the armrest beside him.

Zoey simply shook her head. "No, he didn't. Evie said as much after the funeral. She said he was glad I had joined the Army and wasn't his problem anymore. He was just tired of all the things I got into... All the things he had to clean up." Zoey just stared out the window as she spoke, but Gabe saw a flash of tears before she quickly wiped them away. "I wish I knew how to stop being a burden to everyone I love."

Gabe's heart broke for the little girl who joined the Army because she thought her dad wanted her gone. And it shattered all over again for the woman who sat beside him, still broken because of what was said years ago. He squeezed her hand tighter and said, "He loved you, Zoey. He loved you a lot."

"He was tired of me. He was tired of raising me." She pulled the jacket back up to her chin and pulled her feet up again, but she didn't let go of his hand.

"I had stepsons once, and I will tell you that no matter what your kid does, you still love them. Parents always love their kids," he soothed her, rubbing his thumb across the top of her hand when she finally looked at him.

"Some parents also leave their kids behind and never come back," Zoey sighed. Then she asked, "Where are your kids then?"

"They're in California with their mom and their new dad. I talk to them every so often, and their new dad is a good guy. They're happy, and I don't want to be in the way, so I leave them be. I love them enough to know they don't need me now." Gabe's marriage had fallen apart after five years. He'd been in Afghanistan when the divorce came through. Not that he hadn't known the marriage was mostly over before he left, but leaving had ended it completely. Since then, he had only seen the boys once. They were happy with their mom and stepdad, who was an accountant and home every night with them. Something he had never been.

Zoey didn't have a sassy comeback, so they sat in silence for the next few minutes as Gabe drove. He held Zoey's hand until he saw she had fallen asleep. She slept as soundly as she had the previous night.

CHAPTER 11

It was the quiet that woke Zoey again from her sleep. The rumble of the SUV had seduced her into slumber and had kept her there for hours. Now, it was quiet… Too quiet. She slowly opened her eyes to see Gabe across the car, watching her. She was still tightly holding his hand but dropped it as she sat up straight and rubbed her hands over her face and asked. "Did I fall asleep?" Judging by how light it was outside, she knew she had.

"You got about three hours in," Gabe said dryly from across the car. She could tell that he was shifting around in his seat uncomfortably and assumed he just needed to get out and stretch.

"Well, I'll go then." Seeing Evie's house just down the road, she tossed off his jacket and grabbed the door handle to leave.

"Not yet," Gabe growled. His tone sent a shiver up her spine. Raising an eyebrow, Zoey stopped and turned to face him again. "We have to talk."

"About what? We hardly know each other. We have nothing to talk about." Zoey tried to deflect the conversation but couldn't take her eyes off of his.

"Zoey, you cannot run in the middle of the night," Gabe insisted. Man, he sounded like a broken record.

"But if I stopped running at night, you wouldn't pick me up and take me home." Zoey lightly touched his arm, but quickly dropped it back to her lap at his instant scowl.

"I won't be picking you up tomorrow night. I don't work nights again until next month," his voice was harsh as he said the words. She could tell something was wrong.

"You won't be out there to pick me up?" Her voice came out as a panicked whisper. It had only been two days, but she was relying on him to pick her up. She had tried to convince herself she just needed to clear her mind, but her heart did a small flip whenever she saw his cruiser.

"No, I have four days off, and then I'm on the day shift for three weeks. I don't want anyone else picking you up, Zoey. You don't know what could happen to you." His voice was softer now, pleading.

"I have some idea what could happen," she whispered, trying to lighten the mood. "Maybe I'll be picked up by another cop."

"I wouldn't trust the cops as much as you once did. You're not a kid anymore," he warned, sure he liked everyone he worked with, but there were some that he didn't trust in certain situations. And Picking up Zoey in that outfit would certainly be a situation.

"I don't think there would be a problem. They're all nice guys," she tried to wave off his concern.

"Zoey, you're adorable." He shook his head as he reached over and touched a curl that was resting on her forehead. "They're all nice guys until they have a half-naked twenty-something sleeping in their car. Then they won't be able to keep their hands off you." He tucked the curl behind her ear, and Zoey watched his eyes grow dark as the curl came loose again. When his eyes did that, she wanted to crawl into his embrace and never leave.

"What're you talking about? I'm perfectly dressed," she whispered, her eyes locking with his. Sighing as she felt his hand drift from behind her ear, then down her neck and to her shoulder. He left a trail of fire where he touched her, causing a hitch in her breath when his hand found the top of her breast. Gabe closed his eyes for a moment, not moving his hand any further. When he opened his eyes again, they resembled a stormy bay. Zoey could see something more in them as well.

"Zoey, I can see your nipples through your shirt, and it's been killing me all night," he whispered huskily.

Zoey jerked away from his hand and covered her breasts with her hands. She could feel the heat rushing to her face. "I'm so sorry. I-I didn't know," she stammered and then fled the car. She started to run to Evie's house in the distance, hoping he wouldn't follow. Instead, she heard him slam his door and call her name.

"Zoey! I have your phone!" His yell penetrated her embarrassment, stopping her in the road. She needed her phone, and she needed to go back. With a stiff resolve, she grabbed her breasts with her hands again and turned to walk back to get her phone from Gabe. She wasn't going to give him another show. He met her halfway, holding out her phone her. Fortunately, his eyes were looking at her face, not her breasts in her hands. How was she going to grab it without flashing him? Zoey groaned to herself. She was going to have to flash him again to grab her phone, wasn't she?

Gabe solved the problem by sliding the phone into the pocket of her shorts for her. He kept his hand around the phone in her pocket, then took a deep breath and said, "Please don't run at night, Zoey. Call me, and we can talk instead. You have my number."

Zoey felt the warmth of his hand in her pocket through the thin material of her shorts. Was his hand shaking, or was that her? She could barely hear him over the roaring of her pounding heart. Her leg felt cold once his hand left her pocket. His hand that had held the phone then reached up, and he gently ran his thumb over her cheek. She closed her eyes at the tender touch and waited for his lips to find hers, but in an instant, his hand was gone. Opening her eyes, she watched him walk back to his car. Embarrassment washed over her all over again as she turned and ran the short way back home.

She was happy when she made it to the house, and Evie wasn't up yet. Zoey made it to her bedroom without having to deal with another lecture, and probably a second one as well, if Evie saw what Gabe had seen. Zoey peeled off the offending garment, throwing it into the garbage can in the corner of the bedroom. She never wanted to see that shirt again.

CHAPTER 12

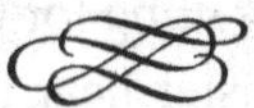

THE SUN WAS hot as Zoey waited on the tailgate of Evie's pickup for her sister to signal that she needed more seed. For the last two days, the two of them had been planting corn over most of the land that was their father's farm. It had been hard work, dragging around fifty-pound bags of corn day after day, then dumping them into the corn planter every three hours. Evie drove the tractor the entire time, so when Zoey wasn't filling the corn planter, she was cleaning out their dad's house or working on weeding their eight large vegetable gardens.

It had been three days since she had last seen Gabe, and the thought of him seeing her through her shirt still made Zoey flush with embarrassment. He had probably been able to see her breasts for hours.

The next night she had tossed and turned, remembering the way his eyes darkened as he looked at her. When she had finally fallen into a light sleep, she was haunted by nightmares again, only to bolt awake and staying that way until dawn. She forced herself not to run to escape the memories. Okay, she had run a little, but only down the road a bit to her father's house so she could get it cleaned out. Zoey had spent the darkest hours of the night dealing with the clutter and had returned every other night to do the same. Now most of the rooms were mainly empty at this point. The furniture would have to go next, but that would take more than one person to handle.

Evie's tractor stopped across the field from where Zoey was parked at. Curious, she jumped down from the tailgate and drove across the field to her sister's tractor. When she got there, she pulled on a pair of work gloves and jumped out of the truck, but found Evie talking to a man parked on the road, not waiting for the seed or broken down.

Deciding to wait for her sister near the pickup because she didn't want to join in, Zoey assumed that Evie was chatting with one of their neighbors. It had been eight years since Zoey had been around, and she couldn't remember all their neighbors, anyway.

Deciding Evie wasn't coming back, Zoey knew she should go say hi to whoever it was. He was taller than Evie, but most people were, and he was leaning against the truck. She saw them shaking hands as she walked up the grassy ditch, and once she got to the road, her heart did a little flip in her chest as she recognized the man as Gabe Watson. Today he was in jeans and a gray t-shirt that was stretched tightly across his broad chest. He was way better-looking in street clothes than in his uniform, and Zoey couldn't help but take in every inch of his lean figure as Gabe leaned against his truck.

He gave her a quick glance as she approached, then went back to talking to Evie. Zoey was instantly jealous of her older sister and his attention. Shocked, she wondered why she even cared—he was nothing to her. Well, nothing but a safe place on a dark night, but then right now, he wasn't even that.

At that moment, Zoey wished she had taken more time to groom herself. She had no makeup on and was covered head to toe in dust and dirt from the house and the field. It was exactly how she had looked every day, but suddenly she wished she had tried to stay cleaner. Reaching up, she touched her hair as she approached them. God, she probably looked terrifying.

"Zoey, do you remember Officer Watson? He stopped your fight with the Jensen boys," Evie explained when Zoey walked up to them as if she and Gabe had only seen each other that night a week ago.

"I remember. I think I was winning that fight when you broke it up." She looked at Gabe's perfect blonde hair; no hat when he was off duty. But it was his eyes that caught her gaze. They were not bright blue; instead, they were stormy and reminded her of when he kissed her.

Gabe tore his gaze from Zoey and turned back to Evie. "I was just telling your sister that I don't remember taking your mother to Minneapolis all those years ago. I thought we should get this out in the open if we're all going to live here."

"You've been back for how long now, and you thought this should be done today?" Zoey challenged. There were a lot of holes in that explanation. What was he really here for?

"Just over a year, but it wasn't until I ran into you that I realized what I had done. I didn't even remember it," he said to Zoey before turning to Evie. "I hope you won't hold it against me. I was a young kid heading to war for the first time when I left that day."

"I don't think I can just forgive you, Officer Watson. Maybe it was just a ride; maybe it was more... I don't know," Evie said, but Zoey knew she wouldn't let it go. There'd be no forgiveness for the man responsible for their mother's leaving. Even if he might have just been an innocent bystander, "Zoey, we have to get going while the weather holds. Have a good rest of your day, Officer."

Evie and Zoey headed back down the ditch and back to the tractor. From the corner of her eye, Zoey watched as Gabe pulled away from the truck and called after Evie. "You know, I can help you fill the corn planter."

As he followed the sisters into the field, Zoey couldn't stop the grin. It seemed he wasn't letting Evie's attitude stop him, but stop him from what? She still had no idea what he was doing there. But maybe it was to tell Evie about the late night running. She was sure that her sister didn't know about it. Well, she knew Zoey ran, but not how long she was usually gone when she did.

"We don't need your help, Watson," Zoey hissed at him. The last thing she needed was more time with him to embarrass herself. "We wouldn't want you to get your nice clothes dirty."

He was in front of them before they made it to the pickup and helped Evie onto the back of her truck with an arm of support. Then, he turned to Zoey and grabbed her by the waist to lift her onto the back of the pickup, but not before she felt his entire body pressed to the back of hers and heard him whisper in her ear, "Maybe I like to get dirty." She then yelped as he hoisted her into the bed of the truck, feeling her face flush at his words.

Gabe easily jumped into the truck bed, making the long box Ford seem very small. He took control of the activities the sisters had been managing for two days. "Evie, why don't you relax while Zoey and I get this filled for you? You've been working all day."

Smiling at the officer, Evie looked around and sat on one of the piles of seed bags as Zoey worked to open bags that Gabe poured into the drill. From her improvised chair, she said, "Actually, I've been sitting in the tractor all day. Zoey's the one that has been working on the house and the gardens. And she went for a run before sunup, but I won't say no to a little relaxation."

Gabe was grabbing a bag that Zoey had just opened when his eyes met hers. She shook her head in response to his silent question: Had she run before sunup? No, she had stayed close to home since the last time she saw him. He must have believed her, because she saw relief in his eyes as he lifted the next bag of seed.

"What house?" His words were directed at Evie, but Zoey knew they were concerned about her.

"Our dad's. We have to get it cleaned out so Zoey can move into it. I think we are down to just furniture now, but then we have to redo the floors, paint, and so much more. Then Zoey can *finally* move out on her own," Evie said casually, making conversation. "Not that I don't love having her, but she's an adult now and needs her own space. How about you? Are you living at your parents' place?"

"No, my mom sold the house after dad died. I'm renting the Wilson place down the road," he answered while tipping another bag into the planter.

"Sam Wilson's?" Evie perked up.

"Yep."

"Sam was Julie Wilson's dad," Evie looked at Zoey. Julie had ridden the school bus with them, but she had been way closer to Evie's age. The house he was at was only three miles from Evie's.

The conversation trailed off as Gabe and Zoey focused on filling the corn planter. Zoey was enjoying watching the muscles in Gabe's back flex as he carried and dumped the huge bags of corn. When he reached down close to her to grab another bag, she saw the sweat damping his gray shirt. The task wasn't as easy for him as he made it seem.

"I've heard some of the stories about Zoey when she was young. Do you worry she'll fall into her old ways?" He was back for another bag of corn and looked into Zoey's eyes again. Without missing a beat, he was gone after picking up yet another bag.

Evie was silent a bit, and Zoey saw her eyes were closed as she leaned against the cab from her corn chair. "Some days, I wish that Zoey would come back. The Zoey who came home doesn't have the spunkiness of the old one, and I miss that spunkiness."

Zoey opened another bag as a tear rolled down her cheek at her sister's words. Gabe was reaching for the bag but, instead, wiped the tear away when Evie was looking elsewhere. "Give it time, Evie, the old Zoey is in there. She'll make it back out." He grabbed a bag and was gone.

Before she could get another bag ready, she felt Evie's arms around her. Her sister held her tight. "I miss you," Evie whispered into her hair.

Zoey hugged her back tightly and said, "I miss me, too." They stayed that way for a moment until Evie pulled back and wiped her eyes on her sleeve.

"The drill looks full. I better get going." Evie jumped off the back of the truck and onto the ground. Zoey watched as her sister climbed into the cab of the tractor and pulled away.

"You made her cry." Zoey angrily wiped the tears from her own eyes before turning to face Gabe. "You made my sister cry."

"Are you going to hit me?" Gabe jumped to the ground.

"No, I don't fight anymore," she said with sadness in her voice. He reached up to help her down as she stood on the back of the pickup and took off her work gloves, throwing them into the bed. Ignoring his offered hand, she sat down on the tailgate to get down herself, but before she could get off the tailgate, he had his hands on her waist and was pulling her to him. He pulled her to the edge of the tailgate and then slowly slid her down his body until her feet touched the ground.

"I don't want to fight with you," Gabe whispered into her ear as he still held her close.

A chill ran down her spine at his words, and she let herself lean into his body. His warmth engulfed her as one of his hands let go of her waist and ran up her back, sending shivers of pleasure through her. With her nestled so close, she could feel his erection through the many layers of clothing that separated them. Burrowing closer, she tried getting closer to him and his heat. She wanted him to kiss her so bad… would he kiss her this time?

Meeting his gaze, she saw the desire there and knew her face held the same look. She licked her bottom lip in anticipation as she felt him take a deep breath. Closing her eyes, she leaned towards him to taste his lips.

Instead, he pulled away. "I have to go."

His warmth was gone, leaving her wanting. Not wanting to watch him go, she kept her eyes on the dirt surrounding her feet. Maybe if she wished hard enough, it would swallow her up. She heard his truck start and drive away in the distance, but still, she stayed where she was. Zoey leaned against the tailgate and thought to herself, *What the heck is wrong with me?* He wanted her, that she knew, but then he just… left. *Whatever it is, it's obviously bad enough to turn him off*, she decided as she pushed off the tailgate to get back to cleaning the house. She didn't need him, anyway.

CHAPTER 13

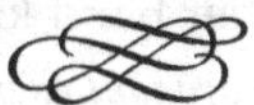

She needed him. She needed him *so* badly.

Zoey paced around her bedroom after waking up from less than an hour of sleep. Now she couldn't even sit down. She desperately needed to get out of the house. After three nights of barely any sleep and constant nightmares, she needed to feel safe again. She needed him because being with him was the only place that seemed to help anymore.

Shaking her head, she changed from her pajamas into blue jogging pants and a matching tank top. *Thanks, Della, for the matchy-matchy exercise clothing*, she thought. Quietly, she headed out of the house, deciding that she would go to her house and work on the paperwork drawers she still had to go through.

Once she made it to her future mailbox, she felt that running was going to help her more than paperwork ever would, so she simply kept going. Turning up her music, Zoey let her mind go as she ran. No thought was put into the direction or the distance; a clear mind was the only goal. She'd run until she couldn't run anymore.

It wasn't until she was in front of Gabe's house that she realized where she was. The small rambler was set off the road a bit, separated from it by a sizeable yard. When she was younger, the Wilsons always had horses betwreen the house and the road, but the fence was gone.

Her feet were on autopilot, and began taking her up the driveway. *Go home*, her mind screamed, but her feet kept bringing her closer and closer to his house. Maybe he wasn't alone—had he mentioned a wife or a girlfriend? What was she even going to say? What would he think about her just showing up?

She heard rather than felt her hand knocking on the door. *Go home, Zoey!* Her mind insisted. *What are you even doing here?* Too late, the door was opening, and there he was, all rumpled and sexy. Gabe leaned against the doorway, wearing only a loose pair of sweatpants. Slowly, she raked her eyes up his chest, noticing a whirl of light hair and a scar resembling a spider web of red lines covering his right shoulder. His blond hair was a mess, just like she had dreamed it would be. Zoey couldn't breathe—she wanted to do all sorts of things to him, yet she desperately wanted to run away.

"Uh, hi," was all she could force from her throat.

"Hi," he answered with a lazy smile.

"This will sound crazy, okay?" She needed to explain, hoping he would understand and not send her home. "I can only sleep when you are around, and I haven't slept in days. I need sleep."

He opened the door wider and motioned her to come in. "I understand."

"No sex, I'm not here for sex," she said maybe too loudly

"I understand, Zoey," he said again, shutting the door behind them.

"I can sleep on the couch. Is your wife here?" She tried not to panic at the thought. They had kissed more than once—nothing much, but enough that a wife would not approve.

"No wife; sleep wherever you want." His back was leaning against the closed door, hands in the pockets of his sweatpants.

Now that she was there, the rest of her non-plan was showing. She wiped her sweaty palms against her running shorts. "Could I take a quick shower?" She knew she was asking too much, but she was sweaty from her run. *He's going to kick me out at any moment*, she thought, because she would have kicked her out already.

"Sure. Bathroom's this way." Pushing off the door, he motioned her to follow him down the short hallway. "I'll grab you a shirt to sleep in; you can't sleep in that. I like it the best of all the outfits I have seen you in, though. Blue looks good on you."

"It's my sister's. Della's a redhead like me. Or she was, it's brown now… But she knows what colors work on us." *Too much information, Zoey,* she chastised herself as she hurried into the bathroom. Turning on the water, she quickly stripped out of the blue running outfit and climbed naked into the shower.

It was sheer exhaustion that forced her to turn off the water and get out of the warm shower. As she dried off, she saw two of his shirts sitting by the sink that hadn't been there when she had entered the room. One was a plain white t-shirt, and the other was gray. Remembering the other night in his car, she immediately grabbed the gray one, not wanting to have that conversation again. Once she had it on, she noticed what it said: Marine. One day, she would make him wear an army one in retaliation, but tonight, she was too tired for that fight.

Leaving the bathroom, she went back to the living room, but it was empty. She saw a light at the other end of the hallway and went to it. Gabe was in there, still with only his sweatpants on, and he was making a bed. Zoey watched his hips as he bent over to tuck a sheet back into place. *Is he wearing anything under those?* He caught her watching him and smiled. "You should have been a Marine, red."

Zoey shook herself out of the trance and grinned back, looking down at her shirt. "I think they spelled 'Army' wrong." When she glanced back at Gabe, his eyes were dark again. God, she loved making him look at her like that.

"Okay, I made up the bed for you. I'm across the hall if you need me." Pausing at the door, he turned and said, "And if I had a wife, I would never have kissed you." Then he hurried out of the room.

Alone again, she looked around for a moment before gently sitting down on the bed. Actually, she collapsed on the bed out of pure exhaustion. She didn't bother to turn off the lights—she couldn't sleep in the darkness, anyway.

Lying in bed across the hall from Gabe, she waited for sleep to overtake her. Nothing. Looking around the unfamiliar room again, she saw only a bed and dresser. Nothing on the walls, and only a lamp on the nightstand. No knickknacks or anything personal; the walls were even a stark white.

Sitting up, she quietly turned off the light and left the room. She should just go home. Heading out of the bedroom, she noticed Gabe had left his light on. Peaking in his bedroom, she saw he was sleeping on his side, facing the door. God, he looked so good, even in sleep. His hair was sticking out in every direction, and it was gorgeous. She wondered if it waited all day to finally be free of its structured life.

Silently, she walked into the room. *Are you crazy?!* she wanted to yell at herself, but she was too tired to stop. Quietly and slowly, she climbed into the empty side of the bed and curled into a small ball.

Just as she was relaxing, he turned over and gathered her into his arms, a sound of contentment rumbling in his chest. She stiffened again, but then sighed as her body melted into his warmth, his smell. In the darkness, their hands clasps just as he kissed her hair and said, "I'll protect you from everything, Zoey. Let me do that for you tonight." Then she thought he had kissed her neck, but she couldn't be sure. She was safe and asleep within minutes.

CHAPTER 14

WHEN GABE WOKE up the next morning, his bed was empty. *Had she even been there?* The shirt she had worn was folded and lying on the end of the bed. Sitting up, he grabbed it and brought it to his face—it smelled like apples…like Zoey.

The side table light was off; she must have turned it off when she had left. Having noticed that she didn't turn off the light in the spare room last night, he had left his light on in case she needed him. He was well aware of how darkness can be the enemy after war.

Gabe got up and threw the shirt back on the bed, deciding it was better she had left before he woke up. If she had been in his bed this morning, he didn't think he could've stopped himself from making love to her. It had nearly killed him to walk away from her twice without kissing her beautiful mouth. She had given him silent permission, but he wouldn't allow it to happen. She was just a kid, and he was old enough to know better.

Why had he even stopped to talk to the sisters the day before? Giving a woman a ride over twenty years ago was nothing to apologize for—a ride he barely remembered. He didn't owe them anything. But he saw them out in the field and had to see Zoey; see her and make sure she was okay.

Then things had gotten out of control, and he wanted to make love to her right there in the middle of a dirt field. He groaned at the memory of her upturned mouth, waiting for him. Her serious brown eyes had been closed, lashes fanning out over her cheeks. She was giving him everything she had to offer, and it took everything he had to walk away.

She deserved better than him, someone closer to her age. But who was he trying to kid? He didn't want to see her with someone her age or any age—*he* wanted her.

Gabe padded across the hall and headed to the shower. He had to work today. Maybe work could take his mind off the unforgettable redhead who had shared his bed last night.

From the way she acted the night before, he knew she was a long way from being over the horrors of war. If she didn't talk, she wouldn't be able to get over it. Maybe next time she would open up, but even if she didn't, Zoey would always be welcome when she needed him. Even though his body wanted more, his mind knew she needed comfort right now more than anything.

* * *

ZOEY WAS glad that she had made it home before Evie woke up. Dragging herself from Gabe's strong arms and warm bed had been an incredible test of her will. What would've happened if he had woken up first? Would she still be there, but making love to him as the first light of dawn spilled through the windows? She knew she wouldn't have been able to say no to him—her body craved his too much.

Once Zoey had showered, she headed down the stairs to start the day. Corn planting was finished, and Zoey didn't know what Evie had planned for them next. Luckily, she didn't have to wait long to find out. Evie was sitting at the table reading the paper when Zoey made it to the kitchen. Evie flashed a warm smile at her before turning back to the paper. "Morning."

"Morning." Zoey poured herself a cup of coffee and sat down across from her sister. "Where's Ben?"

Evie casually replied, "He's already on the bus."

Zoey sat holding the cup, warming her hands and basking in the delicious hazelnut smell that came from the cup. "What's on the agenda today?"

"We are getting rid of most of the furniture today. Farm work first, though, then house stuff." Evie folded the paper closed. She looked at her baby sister and her cup of coffee. "I watch you pour a cup of coffee every morning, but I've never seen you drink it. Do you even drink coffee, Zoey?"

Zoey looked quickly down at the offending cup as if she had never seen it before. Then she looked up at her sister's green eyes and shook her head. "No, I just like to feel its warmth."

"Should I be worried about you leaving the house in the middle of the night? Compared to Afghanistan, Birch Cove might seem safe, but it isn't the best place at night," Evie questioned quietly, still looking into Zoey's eyes, but wrapping her hands around Zoey's over the coffee cup.

"I'm fine. I just need to clear my mind sometimes, and running helps," Zoey mumbled, almost to herself. "One day, I'll be okay."

"Can you please tell me when you're okay, so I can stop worrying so much about you?"

"I will, I promise." Zoey smiled. She hoped that day was coming soon, but feared it was a long way off.

* * *

ONE WOULD THINK that after a long day of moving heavy furniture out of the house and into Evie's truck, and then off the truck and into the landfill, Zoey would be tired enough to simply pass out and get some sleep. But no such luck, so here she was, walking up Gabe's driveway in the dead of night again. She was less nervous tonight, knowing he was waiting for her. Well, not *waiting*, but he had sent a text at around ten that his door would be unlocked. That was an invitation, so it wasn't like she was just barging in.

As she drew nearer to the house, she saw a light on in what she knew was the bathroom, and another in the master bedroom. Had he left one on in the spare room, or did he think she would end up in his room again tonight? Did he know she needed him next to her? That it wasn't the same unless he was right there?

Quietly, she opened the door and closed it behind her, then kicked off her shoes and walked barefoot into the bathroom. The gray shirt was sitting beside the sink again. No white one this time, just the gray one. Zoey couldn't help the shy smile pulling at her lips.

She took her time in the shower, eventually getting out to dry off. Zoey closed her eyes as she slid the shirt over her head. It smelled just like him…laundry soap, and him. She didn't remember the shirt smelling that way yesterday. Was it because she had been so tired?

She shut the light off when she left the bathroom, entering his room quiet as a mouse and hoping not to wake him. Zoey climbed into the bed and under the covers, then curled into her usual ball. Just as she was starting to relax and feel comfortable, Gabe rolled over and pulled her into his arms again.

"You're early," he said into her hair.

She looked at the clock beside her head. "It's midnight."

"I usually don't see you until after two. Midnight's early," He held her tighter.

"I can come back later," she huffed and tried to pull out of his arms, but they only tightened around her.

"Stay," he said firmly. "Maybe you can get a few more hours of sleep in tonight."

She lay silently in his arms, just feeling the comfort and safety of being close to him again. The warmth of his body seeped into hers, and she felt herself relax again. She heard him say, "Goodnight," but fell asleep before she could answer.

CHAPTER 15

Zoey kept an eye on the approaching rain clouds as she finished weeding around the small tomato plants. It hadn't rained in days, so Evie and Zoey had started watering the gardens yesterday. Hopefully, the weather meant that she'd no longer have to stand out with a hose for an eternity. The clouds soon stole the last of the evening light Zoey was working in, so she gave up on the little green weeds and headed to the house.

It had been almost two weeks since Zoey had first gone to Gabe's at night to sleep. Almost two weeks of working all day and sleeping in Gabe's arms at night. She was happy to say that she was…happy. Zoey loved the farm and all the work it entailed, so much so that she was able to get past Evie, bossing her around like she had when they were younger. She was finally becoming confident with her new life; things she hadn't thought about in years were coming back to her. Evie had even let her drive the tractor a few times, which was a *big* deal for her older sister.

Her days were going great, and her nights were even better. Every night she would show up, shower, and climb into bed wearing his gray Marine shirt. She'd sleep for hours that way. Gabe never put any moves on her; he just gathered her into his arms and held her. Then

69

they would talk until she fell asleep, even when it took an hour or two. They talked about everything and nothing at all, staying away from their times at war, and the nightmares that kept Zoey awake at night. She wasn't ready, and he respected that.

It had been odd that sleep was her issue, since five to six hours had always been long enough for her. Because of that, she could sleep and still be able to get up before he did. So far, she had managed to do that every morning.

Though she didn't know where she and Gabe were heading, she knew she would miss him and their talks when it was over. Knowing that their current arrangement couldn't last, she hoped it would at least hold out long enough for her to get over the past; long enough that she would be able to sleep when he was gone.

Walking into the house, she saw that Evie was doing the dishes. Zoey knew she should have come in earlier to do that for her sister— Evie deserved a break. Pulling off her boots, she called out, "I can do that, Evie. You go sit down and watch TV."

Evie did almost everything, and Zoey noticed it. She hated to see her sister working herself too hard, and in the last few weeks, she had noticed Evie didn't eat much and worked too many long hours. The woman was always doing something, either working the farm, working in their dad's house, cleaning her house, or taking care of Ben. She never really stopped.

"I'm almost done," Evie brushed her off as she pulled the plug on the sink. "Did you get the tomatoes weeded?"

"Yes, that garden's done for this week. I think we have to change to bigger cages for the tomatoes next week, though," Zoey stated, hoping Evie didn't see it as taking charge. She wasn't ready for that yet.

"Yeah, I was thinking that too," was all Evie said as she dried her hands. "The truck keys are on the rack over there."

Zoey turned to look at the mentioned keys, but she already knew where the keys were kept—they had been kept there her entire life. "I know."

"I don't want you out tonight in the rain; it's supposed to storm. Drive where you have to go." Evie quickly turned and left the room.

Zoey was left alone in the room, staring at the doorway her sister had rushed out of. Evie knew that Zoey had no way to get around without her sister's pickup. Zoey followed Evie into the living room, where Ben was watching TV. Leaning down behind her sister on the couch, Zoey whispered, "Thanks, Evie."

"No problem," Evie said.

Zoey didn't even know what Evie thought she was doing, but her sister was willing to let her do it without any questions. Maybe she was seeing Zoey as an adult, even if she treated her like a kid all day.

Evie turned to face Zoey. "I think we have to start looking for something for you to drive."

Curious, Zoey sat on the other end of the couch. "Maybe a little car. Something like Della's?"

Evie just looked at her and laughed. "No, no cars. You're a *farmer*, Zoey, you'll need a pickup. If we split up, we can do two farmer's markets in the cities, and you'll need your own pickup to do that. I'll talk to Jeff Teller tomorrow; he sells cars in town now."

Zoey couldn't remember who Jeff Teller was, but Evie trusted him, and so would she. Zoey had a hard time thinking she would fit in a giant pickup like Evie did. She was even shorter than her older sister, and Evie was small in the giant cab. But she was excited about the idea, having never owned her own vehicle before.

For a while, they watched TV without saying much until Evie took Ben up to bed. After half an hour, Zoey realized Evie wasn't coming back down. *She must have gone to sleep early.*

It had started to rain since she had come into the house. She watched a few shows about people buying expensive houses and wondered if she should remodel the kitchen of her house before she moved in. After the couple on the TV picked the most expensive house, Zoey got to her feet and headed to bed. She had another busy day tomorrow, but her feet lead her into the kitchen and to the key rack by the door. She grabbed the keys to the truck and headed out into the rain.

After driving for a few miles, she turned the pickup towards Gabe's place. She stopped the white pickup beside Gabe's and jumped out into the rain. Running, she made it to his door just as he was opening it for her. The rain was coming down good enough that she was already soaked, so she kicked off her muddy boots at the door and went to his bathroom without saying a word to him.

Drying off her hair in the bathroom after stripping out of her clothes when she heard a soft knock on the door making her freeze as the door started to open. *Was he coming in?* She *wanted* him to come in, but watched him slowly open the door just enough for him to put a shirt on the countertop for her. A brief glance told her it was the shirt she always wore—his Marines shirt. After just a second of hesitation, Gabe softly closed the door again, and Zoey released the breath she hadn't realized she'd been holding.

She couldn't believe she had thought he was coming in. He didn't think of her in that way; he was just being nice to her. After pushing all of her pent-up desire back down where it belonged, she walked out of the bathroom. Gabe was in his bedroom, taking off his shirt. He looked at her and grinned. "You're early again. It's just after ten—two hours early. I'm not ready for bed yet."

"I could go and come back later if it helps…," she said the words, but didn't move from the doorway to his bedroom. She couldn't get her legs to move, and she was fairly certain that her brain had short-circuited. Gabe had started unbuttoning his pants, and she couldn't take her eyes off him.

"No," he said, stopping what he was doing. "Get in bed. I'll be back in a moment."

Quickly, he walked past her and out the door, leaving her alone in the bedroom. She still couldn't move. Once she heard the bathroom door shut behind her, her legs finally started moving, and she climbed into what was now her side of Gabe's bed.

Tucking herself deep into the covers, Zoey tried to dislodge the image of him undressing in front of her from her mind. He was *not* hers, and he did *not* find her attractive, anyway—they were just friends. He was just being nice to her because he understood what she was going through.

The bathroom door opened a second later, and she slammed her eyes shut. She had the image of him half-naked burned in her mind already and didn't trust herself to not do something…stupid.

Climbing into bed beside her, he didn't gather her into his arms. He just laid on his back, staring at the ceiling, when he asked, "You drove over?"

"It was raining," was all she said in a way of explanation.

"I had hoped you wouldn't run over here in the rain. There's supposed to be a pretty bad storm tonight," he said, still looking at the ceiling.

She couldn't believe they were talking about the weather. "Yeah, that's what I heard."

He put his hands behind his head. "So, how's your house coming?"

"Good, we got all the old carpet out in the last few days, so we'll be getting new flooring soon." She actually had no idea when they'd get new flooring.

"Carpet or hardwood?" He kept asking questions.

"Definitely hardwood."

"Huh. When do you think you'll be able to move in?" He finally turned onto his side and looked at her, propping himself up on his elbow.

"In about a month, I think. I will still need to paint and buy furniture." Oddly, she found herself finally relaxing, even though his arms weren't around her.

"Are you excited?"

"Yes, and no," she shrugged. "I want to live alone, but I've never actually done that before." She yawned and added, "I don't know if I'll get lonely."

"You get used to it." Zoey could tell he was looking at her, but she wasn't looking over at him. She was staring at the ceiling.

"I don't know. Might be hard." She yawned again and turned towards him with sleepy eyes. He took her hand in his and held it between them.

"I think once you get the house in order, you'll be ready," he whispered. She didn't answer but heard him say, "Goodnight, Red," just as quietly.

CHAPTER 16

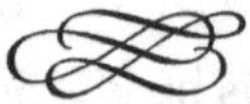

THE DISTANT THUNDER jolted Gabe awake instantly. The storm was now close. Rubbing the sleep from his eyes, he turned and watched Zoey sleep—she was sweating. Even in the dark, he could see the drops of sweat beading on her forehead. Gabe had seen her after running for miles, and she had never been like this. Gabe's heart immediately sunk —she was in the middle of a nightmare, and he knew it. As if on cue, Zoey started pushing against him in her sleep.

"Zoey, babe, wake up," he said as he touched her shoulder and shook her to wake her up. "Zo—"

Before he could get her name out, she pushed him away and scrambled backwards, only to get tangled in the sheets, falling onto the floor. She then immediately scurried backwards until she ended up in the corner of his bedroom. Gabe knew falling off the bed wouldn't wake her—she was still trapped in a nightmare.

Gabe jumped out of bed and followed her. Her eyes were wildly looking around, but he knew she wasn't seeing his bedroom. Her mind was seeing somewhere else, somewhere from her past. Fighting back tears of his own, Gabe grabbed her around the waist with both arms to prevent her from hurting herself even further, knowing she'd push, pull, and fight against him with everything she had. He didn't care—they'd weather this storm together.

Turning and twisting, she almost freed herself, but he tightened his grip and pulled her flush to his chest, holding her as she fought the demons in her past. Gabe's throat was starting to feel hoarse. Without realizing it, he'd been yelling her name over and over, trying to break through to her.

Something must have penetrated her nightmare, because she suddenly went still in his arms. The fight was gone, leaving her breathless and limp.

"Zoey, Zoey, Zoey," he whispered into her ear. "You're okay, you're okay, I have you. I'll protect you." Over and over and over, he whispered the words into her beautiful red hair, her curls soaking up the tears he failed to fight away.

They were leaning against the wall near the corner she had crawled to, Zoey huddling on his lap, and Gabe holding her tight against his chest. He noticed her breathing was becoming less labored, but she had started to violently quake in his arms. Zoey was going into shock. Letting her go with one arm, he reached over to the bed and pulled the comforter around the both of them, then re-tightened his grip on her. But this time with his arms resting against her sweaty body and hers holding tight to him.

Gabe didn't know how long they had sat there like that. He couldn't see any clocks, but knew it had been hours. Holding her, he rocked her in his arms while the thunder and lightning raged outside the window as the storm fully arrived. The loud cracks of lightning didn't seem to affect her now that she was awake. He was still holding her when the storm was gone, and the only sound was the rain on the roof. Eventually, even the rain had stopped, and he still held her tight to him, trying to protect her from the memories in her mind.

"I *will* protect you, Zoey," he promised her quietly. He had no idea how he would do it, but he was determined to, as long as she needed it.

"You can't," he heard her whisper back. It was the first words she had spoken since they had said goodnight, but her voice was hoarse as if she had been yelling all night.

He smoothed a hand up and down her arm. "I know." His mind went back to the look of terror on her face when she made it to the corner and knew she was trapped. He never wanted to see that look in her eyes again. Sleeping or awake.

"Was it the thunder that started it? Is that the trigger?" He wanted to know. It used to be one of his, and maybe still was a little. It was what had awoken him that night.

Not answering for a few minutes, he felt her shake her head in a silent reply.

Quietly, he shared with her. "It was one of mine. When I was first back, I wouldn't even let myself sleep because I didn't want the noise to cause the nightmares to come. The recruiters don't tell you that thunder sounds like gunfire. They don't tell you your buddies will die, either."

"Mine told me I would see the world. See all kinds of places," she whispered numbly.

"Did you?" He hoped she had during his service years.

"I saw a lot of desert."

"Me too. I also saw a couple of hospitals after I was shot." He laughed a little.

"You were shot? Where?" She asked, twisting to look up at him.

"Twice. One in Iraq and one in Afghanistan," he said before adding, "Once in the leg, and once in the shoulder. I'll have to show you my scars one day."

"Is that what the scar on your shoulder is from?" Every night she saw it and had wondered what had happened to cause it.

"Yep. Did you ever get shot?" He hoped she would say no. He didn't want to think about her in that kind of pain.

"No," she answered, and he let out the breath he hadn't even known he was holding. She then whispered, "I would rather have been shot."

"Don't say that," he gently admonished.

"At least you have a scar to prove that something bad happened. When you have no scar, there's no proof." Her arms dropped from his.

He kissed her head. "What happened that left no scar?"

She tensed, and for a moment, he thought she would pull away, but she stayed. After a moment, she dropped her head forward. "I was raped."

That was one of the last things Gabe was expecting to hear. The white-hot rage that surged through his body was instant, and he wanted to kill. He knew she could feel his reaction, but he didn't care. Gabe pulled her closer to his body with one arm and grabbed her hands from her lap with the other. Holding her, he realized her body was shaking again, but this time, she was crying. He soothed her as she cried. "It's okay, it's okay, it's okay."

He could feel her wiping at her tears. "It will never be okay."

"What happened?" He didn't know if she would answer the question, but he knew that if she didn't talk about it now, she probably never would.

She lifted her head and rested it on his shoulder. He watched her shut her eyes as she started to talk. "I had just been promoted to corporal and had been assigned five men to my command. They were all new soldiers…first timers. None had ever been to a war zone before, and a few of them weren't thrilled about their corporal being a female. Some are like that, but I liked the responsibility and knew I would prove myself to them in time."

"I was assigned to a room with a good friend of mine. We'd been there for almost a year together and had a lot in common. I thought we were close. She had also been promoted to corporal and had six soldiers under her. Our careers were finally taking off."

Gabe was silent, soaking in every word. He knew what was coming and hated it. He hated himself for making her say the words and remember the moments she desperately wanted to forget.

"One night, three that were under me, and two that were under her, came to our room. Two hold you down while the rest took turns doing whatever they wanted. They all took their turns with both of us. I remember them holding my head down by pulling my hair. I had it cut off as soon as I got back. It used to be as long as Evie's. But I couldn't stand it anymore."

Pure fury was coursing through his body. It wasn't just rape; it was a gang rape that she had survived. He didn't know how he was keeping himself in check at this point. She needed him to be calm, so he would remain calm for her…for now. "Did you report them?"

Shaking her head, she sniffed, "I shouldn't have,"

"What? Of course, you needed to. They needed to be kicked out of the Army!" He seethed.

"They didn't believe me, Gabe."

"What do you mean?"

"All the guys denied it happened. Laura lied and said it didn't happen either. She knew it would affect her career. So, she stayed in, and I was discharged. Honorably, but still out." Her voice was calm, but he knew that her career had been important to her and had ended because of this.

"They were wrong. Everything that happened was wrong. You know that, right? That's not the way it should've happened." Gabe was still fuming. He had never thought the military could get anything like this so wrong.

"It changes nothing. Wrong or right, it changes nothing," she said.

Gabe didn't know what to say, and he knew he couldn't make it better. No wonder she wasn't able to sleep with memories like those.

The alarm clock buzzed from across the room, startling them both. Zoey quickly pulled out of his arms and ran into the bathroom. Gabe got up and threw the comforter on the bed as he went to turn off the alarm. He sat on the bed and waited for her to come out of the bathroom, her words replaying in his mind. He heard the bathroom door open a few minutes later and waited for her to come back into the room, but instead he heard the front door open and close. Getting up, he walked into the living room and watched through the window as she drove down his driveway. Away.

CHAPTER 17

It HAD BEEN two days since Zoey had told Gabe about why she had left the Army, and she hadn't seen him since. She had stayed in her own bed last night, awake and alone till dawn, but at least she didn't have to see the pity in his eyes when she showed up at his door. Pity was the last thing she needed from him right now. She would rather see desire in his eyes than pity. But he didn't see her that way, not anymore.

"Read the directions again." Evie held up two boards and tried to fit them together.

Yesterday, the sisters had ventured into town and bought the hardwood flooring for Zoey's house. Zoey had a hard time being in the large store with so many people, but had managed to make it out without freaking out, so maybe she was getting better about that. Today, they were putting in the floors...or at least attempting to. Neither one of them was any good at following written instructions.

"I don't need to." Annoyed, Zoey dropped the instructions booklet on the floor and picked up two of the boards, waving them at her sister. "They still make no sense! You read them. You're older. You're supposed to understand more."

Evie huffed as she put the boards down and picked up the paper Zoey had dropped. Sitting down along the wall, Evie read as Zoey tried to put the boards together. With a flair, Evie suddenly ripped up the paper. "You're right! Nobody can understand this mess." She threw the paper into the air and watched the pieces softly float to the floor.

"And people say I have a temper," Zoey smirked at her sister. "The blonde just ripped up the only directions we have."

"Ha, ha." Evie rolled her eyes. "You have a temper, and that's why you ripped up the other two sets. I just followed your lead and did away with the last one." She then gestured to the other tiny pieces of paper scattered on the floor.

Zoey sat down against the wall across from her sister. They were sitting in the living room they had grown up in, separated by a pile of boxes, scattered pieces of flooring, and ripped up little pieces of paper. Neither knew what to do next.

Zoey watched Evie twist her wedding ring around her finger with her thumb, which meant that Evie was thinking. Zoey raised an eyebrow at her, hoping Evie would come up with a plan. Since returning to Birch Cove, Zoey had noticed that Evie planned *everything*. No day began without a plan, and no task was started unless the plan for completion was set. So, Zoey just let her plan.

Zoey picked up one of the pieces of wood flooring and looked at it, tracing a finger along its edge. She had fallen in love with the dark color when she had seen it on the display. After looking at many more options, she had gone back to this one. It was exactly what she had wanted. From there, she would paint the walls light colors and get some soft furniture to start her life. Someday, maybe she and her husband would dance on this floor, and their kids would learn to walk on this floor. Why those kids in her mind looked like Gabe, she didn't want to analyze, but she enjoyed the idea, anyway.

Evie's voice brought Zoey out of her crazy thoughts. "Maybe we should just burn them."

Zoey's head snapped to her sister, who had just suggested to burn her perfect flooring, her *dream* flooring. "No! You can't burn them." She pulled the board she held closer to her, hugging it tightly to her chest.

Evie looked at her and started laughing. Then Zoey started to laugh with her until both sisters were laughing uncontrollably as they sat on the subfloor. Neither had heard anybody come into the yard until a figure stood in the open doorway between them.

Zoey's breath caught in her throat at the sight. It was Gabe, her Gabe. He was wearing jeans and a t-shirt again. This time, his shirt was blue, like his eyes. His blond hair was once again perfectly groomed. She wanted to run to him and crawl into his arms, and she wanted to run out the back door to get away from him, but instead, she just sat where she was.

"Evie, Zoey," he greeted the sisters. "What are you two up to? I could hear you laughing from across the yard."

Sobering instantly, Evie stopped laughing and jumped to her feet. "Mr. Watson, what are you doing here?"

"Gabe, please call me Gabe. I was just wondering if you guys needed some help." He looked around the living room, raising a brow in question. "And I think you do."

Evie eyed him suspiciously. "Do you know how to put in wood flooring, Mr. Watson?"

Zoey knew Evie was not calling him by his name on purpose. She still hadn't gotten over Gabe being the driver on their mother's flight from them. Zoey got up, acting as a buffer between him and her sister.

"I do," Gabe said to Evie. Their eyes were locked in battle.

"Well, we don't need help from you, Mr. Watson." Evie dismissed him and walked towards the kitchen.

"Evie," Zoey chided her sister. "Maybe he can show us how to do it and get us started. Then you can kick him out." She was looking into Gabe's blue eyes as she said it, and he was looking back at hers. She saw none of the pity she expected to see there, just concern.

Without breaking eye contact, he silently mouthed, "Are you okay?"

She nodded a silent yes at him. She was as okay as she had been in months. After their talk the other night, she had been feeling better— maybe not sleeping again, but still better.

Evie whipped around as she said, "Fine, but then you leave, Mr. Watson."

"Gabe," he said, now staring at Evie.

"*Mr. Watson,*" Evie responded firmly, hands on her hips now.

Zoey tried to get between what was possibly a pissing contest in her new living room. "Stop! We need help, and he's willing to help! Don't send the only help we have away, Evie."

Evie and Gabe's eyes were on her in an instant. Both muttered 'fine,' and the tension in the room was relieved. Just a little bit. It was going to be a long day with these two.

Gabe picked up a board and asked, "Where are the instructions?"

Evie snorted, and Zoey said, "Everywhere." Sheepishly, she reached down and picked up a pile of them from the floor to place in his hands. Their eyes met as he smiled at the pile of confetti. "One of us seems to have a temper, right, Evie?"

"Mostly you, Zoey. I only shredded one. You did *two*," Evie giggled. Zoey was relieved her sister was becoming a little more relaxed about Gabe being there.

Zoey took the papers back out of Gabe's hands and threw them high into the air. "They made no sense!" As the tiny pieces of paper fell down around them, Zoey watched Gabe's eyes grow dark with desire. She stopped cold as his hand reached out to her hair. Was he going to touch her right there in front of Evie? Was he going to kiss her? Relief and regret filled her as his hand withdrew, holding a piece of the directions that had been in her hair. She was able to breathe again when he dropped the paper and it fluttered to the floor.

"Okay," Evie said behind her. "Time to prove yourself, Watson."

CHAPTER 18

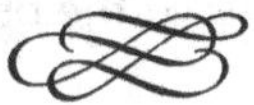

GABE'S KNEES and back were killing him—he had been putting in Zoey's hardwood floors all day. They almost had the kitchen done; earlier, he had finished the living room and bathroom. Leaving just a bedroom without new flooring on this floor. He glanced up at the stairs and wondered what was happening up there flooring-wise—he didn't really want to be the one putting in more hardwoods...unless Zoey asked him to, of course.

The sisters were sitting behind him, laughing about something. He was used to hearing Zoey laugh now. When he had shown up uninvited this morning, his heart did a flip when he saw Zoey sitting on the floor, laughing and smiling. Her beauty took his breath away, and the same breath had been stolen when bits of paper confetti had landed in her hair. Everything in him had wanted to pull her into his arms and kiss her with laughter still clinging to her, just to see what it tasted like. But Evie had been there, and Gabe knew better than to cross the woman, yet.

Gabe had spent the day trying not to touch or look at Zoey for fear her sister would see right through him and his excuses for being there. He had come over to make sure Zoey was okay. He had been worried when she hadn't come to his house for two nights in a row. Now that he knew how bad her nightmares were, he had spent restless nights waiting for her. After seeing her smiling and laughing, he was relieved that her the demons were far off in the horizon today.

"Another long one," he called out, and eleven-year-old Ben came running with a new board. Since the boy had gotten off the school bus, he had been bringing him the wood pieces Gabe had needed. For most of the day, it had been one sister or the other helping him until the boy took over. "Thanks, buddy."

"Sure, Gabe. Tell me when you need another." Evie's son had been quick to warm up to the strange man helping his mom and aunt, much faster than Evie herself. He still felt she was not exactly happy with him being there, but was happy the floor was getting in, so she had let him stay. They had even fed him lunch, but he felt both of them knew that it was slave labor.

Sitting up to rest his back, he leaned against the wall and could see the sisters sitting in the living room. Both were digging into boxes. He knew from their conversations that they were going through their father's stuff, and though the day had been filled with laughter, there also had been some tears. Over the course of the day, he had realized how much their mother's leaving had affected the sisters, each in their own way.

Gabe had found out a lot about the redhead that shared his bed. She was lovingly teased by her sister for being short and red-haired, though based on some of the pictures he had seen, the other sister was a short redhead also. Teasing and laughter was the way the sisters communicated. Zoey was scared of spiders and snakes, but not heights, even though she had a tendency to fall from them. She was also allergic to nuts, and hated most vegetables even though she planned to grow and sell them as a business. Gabe also saw that Zoey would run her hands through her beautiful curls when she was frustrated, and both sisters touched each other's heads or hair lightly when they were making an emotional point.

Gabe saw the concern in Evie's eyes for her sister when she thought no one was looking. Gabe carried the same concern for Zoey, even more now that he knew what was haunting her. He could tell Evie didn't know the details, but that she wanted to.

"Gabe," Ben called him from the living room. Instead of answering, he walked in to see what the boy wanted. "Come sit and look at this, Gabe." Ben was sitting on the floor between his mom and aunt, looking at pictures.

Walking over, Gabe sat down next to the boy, which also happened to be next to Zoey—very close to Zoey. He took the picture from the boy's hand and looked at a much younger Evie holding a baby; she must have been a teenager when the boy was born. She still looked too young to have an eleven-year-old son, but in the picture, she looked too young to have graduated when the picture was taken.

"Is this you?"

The boy beamed. "Yeah, when I was born."

He looked up at Evie. "You must've been young when you had him."

Zoey laughed and answered for her sister. "She's only thirty and has a half-grown kid."

Gabe picked up another picture of three girls standing in a line. There was a definite age difference between the first two and the last one. The youngest one was definitely Zoey, though she had long hair in the picture—all three did. How could Evie be thirty if Zoey was twenty-nine? Was the computer wrong?

"Come on, Ben, we should get home and get you fed." Evie frowned at her son.

Ben scrambled up. "But I was helping Gabe."

Evie shot Zoey a look and said, "Zoey can help him. Supper's ready in an hour."

Gabe and Zoey watched Evie march out of the house with her complaining son following behind. "What was that about?"

"I hit a nerve. She doesn't like to be reminded that she was nineteen when he was born," Zoey said. "I guess we have to get this done in an hour." She went back to the kitchen, grabbing an armful of boards as she headed back out to the living room.

For the first time all day, he could stare at Zoey without worrying about someone watching. She had shed her sweatshirt hours ago and just had a t-shirt and tight jeans on, tight enough that he could enjoy watching her butt sway as she carried her load. Following her, he enjoyed the view.

She dropped the boards gently on the floor, then sat cross-legged near the edge they were working on. He sat down next to her in a huff. "I'll keep that in mind, about Evie's age. I don't need another reason for her to not like me." He took the board she handed him and placed it in its new location.

"She doesn't really seem to like you, huh? She doesn't like a lot of men, so don't feel too special," she smirked as she handed him another board.

He placed the board on the floor. "I thought I was making progress, too. She called me Gabriel once."

Zoey handed him another board as she slid down the floor to a new spot. "I think she called you 'Gabriel Watson.' She probably would've added your middle name if she'd known it." Zoey handed him the next board.

"It's John. You can tell her for next time." He placed the board on the floor, smiling. Evie still may not like him too much, but she was happy with the free labor he had provided. "By the way, how is it that your uniform had your middle name on it? Connor Hart, not just Hart?"

Shifting a little closer to him as she handed him another board, her eyes were on the board as she said, "I legally changed it after boot camp. It seemed weird for people to just call me Hart. Guys in boot-camp made it sound more like an endearment than a last name, and I hated it. Connor Hart broke that up a little. Della changed hers also, but she did it after Dad died to avoid that lecture."

"Do you have another middle name?" He was fascinated by this woman and her life.

"No," she shook her red curls, "all three of us only have Connor as our middle name. Mom wanted us to be a part of her family legacy, even though I've never met a Connor I was related to."

He took another board. "So Evie isn't just Eve?"

"Nope, it's Evangelina. My oldest sister Della's name is actually Delphinea. And then there's me, nothing fancy and fun, just a name with no nicknames at all." She handed him the last board, then wiped her hands on her jeans.

He placed it in its spot with a snap, then turned to her and said, "I think Zoey's fun. You don't have to be fancy." He reached out, touching her cheek as he had longed to do all day. Gabe watched her brown eyes as his hand slid from her cheek to her hair and to the back of her head. With his fingers surrounded by the soft curls, Gabe pulled her head slowly towards him. He felt the pressure of her hands on his legs as she leaned into him. He had tried to be gentle when their mouths touched, but Zoey seemed to have another idea in mind when she softly bit his lower lip.

He let out a groan as she opened her mouth and gave him complete access to it. As he took what she was giving, she crawled onto his lap, and he pulled her close.

Gabe felt a vibration run through them, but ignored it and continued kissing the woman he had been dreaming of for weeks now. When the vibration started up again, he pulled away and looked into her face. She was beautiful, her eyes dark wanting him. "Your phone," she sighed. Ignoring it, her mouth started lightly kissing his cheek and jaw.

"Damn it," he growled. He took the phone out of its holster on his hip, ready to just throw it in the corner and continue with Zoey. He quickly looked at the screen—it was the station. Controlling his breathing, he answered the phone with Zoey still on his lap, but now nuzzling his neck.

"Watson, there's a situation at the bar. You need to come in." The line went dead as the voice hung up.

"Damn it," he said again. "I have to go."

"Work calls," she said as she got off his lap.

"I guess it's for the best. You've been summoned for supper soon." He tried to make a joke, but it fell flat. "And I'm too old to be doing that stuff with you, anyway," he added.

"What stuff?" She asked innocently, but he noticed her tongue slide out and lick her upper lip. When she saw he was watching, she just smiled and winked at him.

"Damn it, woman!" He said as she let out a little laugh. "I'm nearly forty—you are going to kill me."

Mischief was in her eyes when she said, "Almost *forty*? You're right; I might kill you. It would be hard for you to keep up with all this youth. I definitely wouldn't want you to succumb to my youthful *vigor*." She winked at him again and ran a finger slowly across his jaw, then down his body, past his chest and stomach, and then down his fly.

"Christ, woman," he growled. Gabe grabbed her and kissed her smart little mouth. Her adventurous arm and hand were trapped between their bodies, but that didn't stop her from cupping him. Gabe released a tortured moan before he let her go and headed out the door. At the threshold, he turned and asked, just to bring the numbers to light, "How old are you?"

She grinned slyly at him. "Twenty-eight." Shaking his head, Gabe walked out into the chilly night and hoped he'd have his body under control when he got to work. He doubted there would be enough time to climb down from the ledge she'd put him on.

Hours later, when Gabe got home, he was disappointed Zoey wasn't there. He waited in case she showed up, but around two in the morning, he decided to text her. Maybe she was worried he wouldn't be the gentleman she had needed him to be at night now that they had kissed.

You can come here if you want. I won't touch you.

He lay in bed for a few minutes, hoping that maybe she would decide to drive over, but when he heard the ring of a text coming in, he knew she wasn't coming.

That wouldn't stop me from touching you, though.

He groaned at the images racing through his mind. Another ring of a text came through.

Good night, Gabe.

Good night, Zoey Hart.

He couldn't stop smiling as he drifted to sleep. God, he was getting attached to that woman.

CHAPTER 19

IN THE THREE days since Gabe had helped put the flooring in for Zoey. His body had finally recovered from the hard labor, but he was still reeling from the effects she had on his body every time he thought of her. His entire being remembered her taste, her touch.

So far, she still hadn't shown up at his house in the middle of the night. They had exchanged a few texts, and she said was trying to work through her sleeping issues without him. She said it was getting a little easier after she had talked to him that night and had even thanked him for being a good listener and friend. Truthfully, Gabe thought he was an awful friend who wanted nothing but to have her back in his bed again, but this time, naked and under him.

Stopping at the station just before six, he switched vehicles to head home for the day. Another uneventful day in Birch Cove—the best kind of days.

Maybe he could just call Zoey and talk to her, making sure her texts were not just a cover and that she actually wasn't holding up very well. He'd bring up the idea of helping her finish the flooring. But really, he just wanted to hear her voice.

Pulling into his yard, he parked next to a large red truck. After getting out of his pickup, he saw Zoey leaning out the open window and grinning at him. "Hey, copper, like my new truck?"

Walking around his truck to stand outside her window, he leaned on it and said, "It's a little big, don't you think?"

The pickup had twice the power of his and made her look even smaller in the cab. She was simply adorable. And he loved the red. It was more her than her sister's white one.

Her grin didn't diminish, and he could see her brown eyes were dancing with excitement. "You're just jealous because yours is so tiny." The sunlight bouncing off her red hair made it sparkle, just like her eyes.

"You got me, Zoey. I need to trade mine in now—it's too small." He grinned at her.

"Nope, I won't let you. We need something that gets better gas mileage." His heart skipped a beat in reply.

"What's your plan with the beast?" He asked, tapping it with his hand.

"Many, many Farmers Markets. But first, I'm going to take you for a ride in it." She was grinning like a cat that'd got cream.

"Can I change first?" Gabe was still in his uniform, and his gun was still at his hip.

"Put on something pretty for me." She winked at him.

He made it into the house and got ready faster than he had in years, throwing on a pair of jeans and a t-shirt. Yanking open the door, he climbed into the passenger seat.

She was just sitting there, looking at him with a grin on her face. "This is my first car, truck, everything. The bank and I have decided we will co-own it for a while."

He smiled at her, nodding back at his truck. "The bank and I co-own that one as well. We have a lot in common, you and I."

Her hand reached out and touched his hair. "Can I mess this up?" She scooted closer to him.

His breath caught in his throat, and he nodded. "Sure." Even as he said the words, her fingers ran over his scalp and through his hair.

"I've wanted to mess your hair up since you first carried me out of the bar. It was so perfect." Both of her hands were in his hair and running down his neck, pulling him closer and closer.

He grabbed her around the waist and pulled her to him so that she straddled him on the seat. He could tell that she felt his erection pushing back at her by the way she scooted herself closer to it. His hands slid around the top of her jeans and the skin that lay beneath. "I thought you were taking me for a ride?" His voice was hoarse as he asked.

"I am, Gabe, just not on the road." Laughing, she moved her hips against his before nipping at his ear and answered his silent question with a whisper. "Yes, Gabe, in the truck."

He groaned and ran his fingers through her curls, watching as they bounced every which way in the sunlight. Her hands had moved to the bottom of his t-shirt and were pulling it up and over his head. After throwing it in the back seat, she just leaned back and looked at him. Her fingers lightly touched the scar on his shoulder, then her lips followed. Pulling away from his scar, she kissed him on the lips, hard and fast. He got lost in the feeling of her mouth on his and her hands running up and down his chest.

His hands skimmed up her sides until they reached the underside of her breasts—she wasn't wearing a bra again. His hands then slid up the short distance to cup the warm globes in his hands. God, they'd felt better than he had ever imagined they would, surpassing his every fantasy.

With a growl, he pushed her away. "We can't do this in here."

Smiling, she pulled his head back towards her soft lips, now swollen from kissing, but he dodged her. "Why not?"

"Because I don't want to make love to you for the first time in a car, Zoey. I want to go slowly with you." Leaning forward, he nuzzled her neck. "*Very* slowly. I want you burning for me."

Burying her hands in his hair again, she said, "I don't want to go slowly, Gabe. I want you inside me *now*." She bit his shoulder lightly. "Fast, then you can go as slow as you want."

Groaning, he pulled her tight to him, still kissing her delicate neck. He whispered, "Slow, then fast."

With a coy smile, she gyrated her hips on his erection and argued, "Fast, first."

Leaning into his hands, she

filled them even further with her breasts. As if time itself had slowed down, she gently placed her hands on either side of his face and breathed out the word, "Please."

Gabe's eyes flashed with desire, instantly losing any control he had. He kissed her on the mouth hard and fast, and she met him with every move. Without breaking the kiss, he opened the door of the truck and maneuvered them both out of the vehicle. He walked to the house with her legs still wrapped around him, her arms holding him around the neck. As he went to kiss her again, he said into her mouth, "Not in the truck."

She pulled away from the kiss as they entered the house and gave him a coy smile. "Next time." Then she moved her hand from his shoulders to his hair again, and her warm mouth purred against his ear. Gabe made it halfway through the living room when his knees started buckling from the world-shattering sensations she was sending through his body. He stopped and leaned against the wall for support and started to slide down the wall.

When his butt hit the ground, her mouth was back on his, matching his tongue thrust for thrust. The kiss only breaking when he took off her pink t-shirt. Once the shirt had been thrown through the air, he feasted on her glorious, perky breasts. She moved so that she was straddling him again, and he vaguely felt rather than saw her remove her shoes.

He was still suckling first one breast, then the other when she pulled him backwards, and they both landed with a thud on the floor. He was on top of her, their bare chests touching. Gabe could feel her laughing as she said, "Graceful, Hart."

He pushed himself up so he could look into her eyes. She was still smiling, but now it was directed at him. "Let's move this into the bedroom, my graceful Hart."

Grabbing him around the waist, he grunted as she flipped him over. He had forgotten that she wasn't your average woman. He was laughing when she said, "Hot and fast and *right here*."

He easily flipped them both over again. "Slow and smooth and *not* here."

Giggling, she flipped him again, but this time she shimmied down and sat low on his hips so that he couldn't move his lower body. Taking advantage of her positioning, she unbuttoned his pants and slowly slid the zipper down with her teeth. He stopped fighting her as she tugged his pants and underwear down, revealing his pulsing manhood. He watched her eyes grow wide with need when she touched him, delicately wrapping her fingers around his length. Zoey's mischievous eyes never left his as she lowered her mouth to taste him.

With speed and grace, he had her on her back again before her mouth could touch him. "You can't do that kind of stuff if you want fast and hot," he said, knowing he wouldn't be able to last if she took him in her mouth. Quickly, he pulled her jeans and panties from her body and ran his hands over the newly exposed skin. His mouth went back to loving her breasts as his fingers found her core wet and waiting for him. Rubbing gently, a soft growl rumbled through his chest, their eyes locking as the orgasm rocked her body. He loved how her body responded to his touch.

Zoey's body was still pulsing when he found himself flipped on his back again. Lazily, she wrapped her hand around his shaft again and purred, "I thought that wasn't allowed in fast and sexy." She stroked him once, twice, three times, and he closed his eyes, enjoying the sensation of her hands on him.

"I guess I forgot the rules, my Hart." He let the endearment slip from his mouth as he felt her lick his small, hard nipple. His body reacted with a jerk as he sat up, grabbing her head to his chest. She pushed him back down and laughed. God, her laugh made him want to bury himself inside her.

It surprised him when he felt her roll a condom slowly down his shaft. She must have brought it with her. Damn, he loved how she touched him. Then Gabe felt her sweet heat hovering over his shaft. His eyes flew open and looked into hers as she took him all in, watching her soft, brown eyes turn to liquid. He ran his fingers through her wild curls and kissed her deeply, but she pushed him down as she started to move. He watched her eyes slowly close as the pleasure increased.

"Open your eyes, My Hart, I want you to watch us." Zoey's eyes popped open with a gasp as he squeezed her ass with both hands. Their eyes held as they moved, the pleasure increasing and eventually taking them over the edge.

Both were breathless and limp on the floor as she lay on his warm chest. He was running his hands up and down her back, from her hairline down to the roundness of her backside and back up again. "I lied to you, Gabe," she said quietly. His hands stopped their exploring. Lifting her head, she looked at him in his eyes. "I'm not twenty-eight."

Gabe groaned, and his hands started touching her again. "Zoey, Zoey, Zoey."

She rested her chin on his chest, still looking into his eyes. "I'm only twenty-seven." She kissed his chest and looked back into his blue eyes. "next month."

"Damn it," he said as he rolled her onto her back. Zoey released a happy giggle. He kissed the tip of her nose, then her forehead, then nuzzled her neck. His body stirred back into action when her hands started exploring the contours of his back and neck. He simply couldn't get enough of this woman.

Her hands moved to his chest, but they were pushing him away. He quickly leaned away from her to see into her eyes. Was she remembering something from her time in Afghanistan? But when he searched her eyes, they were sparkling. Relief washed through him as the sparkle turned to liquid again, and Zoey said, "Now it's time for slow and smooth."

"You're right." Gabe smiled at this gorgeous, brave woman who meant everything to him. He jumped to his feet and looked down at her small, lean body lying on his floor. Since she was naked, Gate kicked off his shoes, pants and boxers.

As she watched his jeans hit the floor, she said, "Classy, Gabe. You didn't even take your pants off for me the first time. You sure know how to make a lady feel special." Then she let out a loud laugh.

When he was free of his clothing, he held out a hand to Zoey. She grabbed it, and he pulled her to her feet and into his arms for a long kiss. When they finally pulled apart, he said, "Sometimes that happens during fast and sexy, babe. Now for slow and smooth." He picked her up in his arms and carried her laughing to his bedroom.

CHAPTER 20

ZOEY WOKE WITH A START, but it wasn't the usual nightmare that had torn her from sleep. She lay still as she listened for a sound that might have woken her—nothing. Then she noticed Gabe was not in bed beside her. That must be why she woke up. She sat up in the bed and heard him moving around in the other part of the house.

With a smile, she flopped back down on the bed. Stretching, she could almost feel his hands running over every inch of her body again. Making love with Gabe had been better than she had ever imagined. Once they had moved into the bedroom, they had started with the "slow and smooth" version, but that hadn't worked too well and turned into "fast and sexy" again.

She had fallen asleep in his arms, like so many times, but this time, it had felt so much better. So *right*.

Zoey looked up as she heard Gabe walk back into the room, mirroring his smile. He was only in a pair of boxers, leaving his gloriously muscular chest bare. Gabe offered her a plate and a glass of water. "Hungry?"

Sitting up, she used the sheet to cover her naked chest as he put the plate on the nightstand and walked out of the room again. When he came back, he was carrying the t-shirt that she always wore to bed. He handed it to her without a word, then sat on the bed with his back to her, giving her a moment of privacy.

"I'm dressed," Zoey said, and he turned and leaned against the pillow and held out the plate to her. She shimmied up to lean against her pillow and took half a sandwich.

She took a small bite and almost spit it out when he asked, "Are you shy now?"

Chewing slowly, Zoey analyzed the sandwich in her hand. "Just not used to this part."

Gabe put his sandwich back on the plate and studied her. "The after part?"

She wouldn't look at him...she couldn't. Images from the night before flashed through her mind, images of things she had done. Heat and shame rose up in her. "All of it."

Gabe took the sandwich from her hands and, after he put the plate on the table, gathered her in his arms.

She was tense for a moment, but the heat from his body persuaded her to relax into him. "You have nothing to be embarrassed about, Zoey. I loved every moment of it, and I was hoping you did, too."

"I did," she blurted. "It was better than I ever thought it was going to be."

"I thought so, too." He kissed her head.

They stayed that way for a long time as Zoey let go of the embarrassment that had consumed her upon waking. What did she have to be embarrassed about, anyway? He was there just like she was.

"How many 'morning after's' have you had? You don't have to answer if you don't want to." Gabe didn't let her go, he just kept holding her.

"It's okay," Zoey paused before adding, "Willingly and including you?"

"Yes."

"Just one," she said, then whispered, "Just you."

She could hear and feel him groan. She pulled away and finally looked in his eyes. They were dark blue as they stared back at her. "What?"

"Twenty-six and a virgin." He smiled, then kissed her forehead again.

"Not exactly a virgin," she whispered. "I told you…." She let the rest of the words hang in the air.

Pulling her back into a tight embrace, he then pushed her away from him as he took her head between his two strong hands. He forced her to look into his eyes. "Zoey Connor Hart, I need you to listen to me and remember what I am saying to you. That night had nothing to do with sex. That night was about some assholes who couldn't let you have power over them. What they did had nothing to do with sex. When you ever have to tell your sexual history to anyone, that night is not included. Ever."

Zoey couldn't keep the tears from slipping out of her eyes, but she couldn't hide them because of his hands holding her face to his. She watched him as he kissed each tear running down her cheeks.

She lay in his arms, feeling the steady rhythm of his heartbeat and breathing. She thought he had fallen asleep and almost jumped when he said in a near-whisper, "Next time, I promise it'll be slow."

"Sorry, I messed up your plans," she sighed into his chest.

He chuckled. "I had no plans other than to keep my hands off you. I guess *that* plan didn't pan out, but yours was better anyway."

She smiled and hugged him closer to her. "My only plan was to make love to you before I could chicken out, or you ran off again."

"I think I stopped running when I walked in on two sisters who couldn't stop laughing at each other." Without looking at him, Zoey could tell he was smiling. "I love to hear you laugh, especially when I'm making love to you. Which I'm going to do again, by the way. Right now."

Neither of them got any more sleep that night. In the morning, Gabe kissed her goodbye as he headed for the shower, and she headed back to Evie's in her new truck. It was the first time she hadn't left him still sleeping. She liked the change.

CHAPTER 21

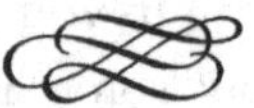

EVIE HADN'T SAID anything to Zoey that morning, but she couldn't help but feel that her sister was disappointed in her. It didn't help that Zoey had no idea what she was going to do without having Gabe beside her at night for a week. Though she had spent a few nights without him, she had always had the option of going to him. This week, that option was out.

When she had told Evie that Gabe was willing to help with the flooring today, Evie had been unimpressed with the idea. She told her that he was even happy to do it, but Evie's only response had been that Zoey could help him, since Evie had too much work to do. Her tone implied that Zoey's contribution to the farm that day had not been needed or wanted.

The tension on the farm was palpable. It hadn't been like this since Zoey's return. She had always felt wanted and needed by Evie, until today, though. Zoey kept her head down, did what she was asked, and didn't question any of it. It was the first time in a long time that she wondered if Evie was going to send her packing.

She had tried to concentrate on work, but her eyes kept drifting to the road, watching for Gabe's pickup truck. It was afternoon before she saw it drive by Evie's farm and turn into hers. Evie hadn't said more than a dozen words to her all day, so without a word to her, Zoey headed to her house.

She parked her truck alongside his and jumped out. Gabe was already in the house, so she walked through the door and into his arms. Just feeling his strong arms around her eased some of the tension she'd been holding on to that day. Their lips met for a long, deep kiss. When it ended, she sighed, leaning her head against his chest.

"Evie coming?" He asked, running his hands through her hair.

"No, she has work to do. You know, unlike me... I don't do anything around here." She couldn't hide the frustration in her voice.

"Then we better get this done so we can prove to her that you're working." He pulled out of her arms.

Working side by side in the empty house made it hard to keep her hands off of him, but she had managed just that for over two hours. Mostly by keeping busy—she even spent time washing her new floor in the other rooms.

Gabe was almost done with the room and was to the point where he didn't need her help anymore. He was working on the small closet in the bedroom that had once been her dad's and would soon be hers. With so little memory of her mom, Zoey had only ever thought of it as her dad's room. She was in the middle of the kitchen with a wet rag in her hand, washing her beautiful new floors. Looking around, she smiled—they were turning out exactly how she had imagined. She watched her sexy lover walk out of the bedroom with something in his hands. It was a picture.

Holding it up, it was of a middle school-aged, red-headed girl to her face and asked, "You or your sister?"

She wiped her hands on her pants to dry them, then took the picture. She looked at the back for writing, but it was blank. Zoey furrowed her eyebrows in thought, then looked back at the front. "Neither. Looks really close, but this girl has blue eyes. I have mud brown, and both Evie and Della have green. I have no idea who this is."

"A cousin?" He asked.

"Maybe, but I've never met any cousins. Evie might know." She looked at the picture again, her face a mask of curiosity.

"Maybe your dad had an affair, and she's a love child," he said, taking the picture from her and putting it on the kitchen countertop.

"My dad, I think, would avoid another redhead like the plague. Mom burned him good. I never even saw him date after Mom left." She started washing the floor again. "Where did you find it?"

He was walking back into the bedroom. "In the back of the closet, stuck in the door frame."

Zoey got up to put her wash bucket in the sink in the kitchen. She wanted to see her new bedroom. "Did you finish?"

"Yep," he said with a grin. "Now, I can do *this*."

He walked up to her, and instead of pulling her to him, he backed her into the wall behind her. His hands went under her t-shirt until he captured her breasts, squeezing them slightly. Zoey couldn't breathe as he stroked his thumbs over her nipples. He had turned her on in a second.

"When are you going to get a nice bed in this room? I can see you naked and screaming for me, holding on to a wrought iron headboard. Can you see it, Zoey? Can you feel it?" His voice was harsh and sent shivers of pleasure from her head to her toes, which were curling.

"Can we try it without the bed?" Zoey reached up and ran her fingers through his perfect hair, making it all stand on end. She felt her shirt lifting off as his mouth took over for his hands. "The floors look nice." She started tugging at the bottom of his shirt.

"They're cold and hard." He had surfaced from her breasts to unbutton her pants and slip them down her hips.

"Beautiful, Gabe. They're beautiful," she whispered as his fingers found her core.

"You're beautiful, Zoey. My beautiful Hart," he murmured back as he suckled her breasts again, moving his fingers in rhythm with his mouth.

Her knees soon gave out from the intense pleasure, sending them both to the floor. She laughed at herself, "Graceful, Hart."

Gabe laughed with her as he pulled his pants off and grabbed a condom from his pocket in one fluid motion, leaving him gloriously naked before her eyes. Running her hands up his thigh muscles and the red scar there, her fingers barely grazed his straining erection, causing his muscles to tense under her fingers. She snatched the condom from Gabe and deftly rolled it down his length, feeling the heat of him in her hands. "My graceful Hart. I love it when you laugh." As he entered her, her laugh turned into a soft moan, and the moan then turned into screams of his name over and over again. *God, he was perfect,* she thought to herself. Zoey wrapped her arms around Gabe's broad back, digging her nails into his skin and imagining wrought-iron headboards.

Her senses came back to her after what seemed a lifetime later, and she found herself held tight in Gabe's arms. Zoey folded her arms on top of his chest, then propped her chin up to look at him. She was lying on top of him on the cold, hard floor, and he was staring at her hair and touching it gently. "I just can't get over these curls. Since the first moment I saw you... No, I didn't actually see them until I had hauled you out of that bar. But once I put you down, I couldn't get enough of them. All these soft, bouncy curls."

If she wasn't already lying down, her knees would have given out on her again. His hand left her hair and touched her cheek, "And your eyes are *not* mud brown, Zoey. They sparkle when you are happy and darken to nearly black when you're turned on." Gabe stared into her eyes intently. "I don't know which color I like better."

To hide her embarrassment at his words, she pushed away from him and grabbed her shirt as she said, "You say the prettiest things about a crazy redhead."

He sat up with her, his face now completely serious. Reaching out, he gently placed a finger against her cheek and turned her head to look at him again. "The words are not nearly as pretty as you are, babe. They don't even come close." He let her go and moved to pull on his pants, and she got dressed beside him. Gabe zipped up his pants, then pulled Zoey to her feet before pulling his shirt on. "And besides, the crazy keeps me on my toes. Or is it off my toes?" He glanced up at his disheveled hair, then threw Zoey a mischievous wink.

Zoey laughed, breaking the tension of what seemed to be part of their after-sex routine for her. She hoped that would stop soon—it embarrassed her as much as her brazen behavior did. Looking around, she tried to find something to do. She caught him staring at her. What was he thinking?

"When are you getting that bed in here?" Gabe whispered low in her ear as he moved behind her. His breath tickled her neck.

Zoey's heart started racing as the images he had planted in her mind earlier flashed through her mind again. Then the ones from the night before flooded her thoughts, mingling with the fantasy of him making love to her in a beautiful wrought iron bed in the middle of her empty bedroom. She bit her lip as the images engulfed her.

"Am I there?" He breathed into her ear, running his hands over the curves of her waist. "Are you picturing the white sheets like I am, Zoey?"

As the fantasy suddenly gained more detail, her breath stopped. In her mind, he was above her in that bed, his body linked to hers like the night before. Their eyes meeting and holding, tuning everything else out completely.

In the harsh light of the naked bulb in the bedroom, he was right behind her, touching her body with his words, but not with his hands. She leaned her head back into his shoulder and nodded. She saw it all, felt it all.

His hand came around and gently encircled her breast, the other hand skimming down her body and into the top of her buttoned jeans. His hand stopped when it came to a stop just inches from where she needed to be touched. Pushing her rear end into him, she silently begged for more.

Hoarsely, he whispered into her ear, "Are you screaming my name, or am I screaming yours?"

The words took her over the edge and a shudder ran through her as her clit pulsed and an orgasm rocked her body. Gabe held her steady as her body reacted to just his words, her thighs squeezing tightly over his hand.

Her breath was ragged when she said, "Oh my God." He was holding her to him with both hands now, fingers splayed across her stomach.

What had she done? Putting her hands to her face, she covered it, hiding the blush that was turning her face as red as her hair. She felt his heat leave her back and pull her hands off her face. When she could see he was standing before her, concern all over him. Gabe's blue eyes were boring holes into her, and she slammed her eyes shut, so at least she couldn't see him.

"No, you can't be embarrassed now," he said. She could tell he was a bit upset.

"I'm so sorry." She didn't open her eyes. "I can't believe I did that. You weren't even touching me," she whispered, more to herself than to him.

"And it drove me *crazy*, Hart. I have no words to tell you how it felt having you fall apart in my arms just thinking about us making love in this room. Can you imagine how good it's going to be when we're actually in that bed if you can feel that deeply before it even happens?"

She cracked her eyes open to look at him. Her embarrassment started to wane at the serious expression on his face. "But I'm not good at this."

He pulled her into a huge hug. "You are great at this, Zoey. You're better at this than anyone I've ever been with. The way your body reacts to mine amazes me every time I touch you." He pulled back so he could see her.

Their eyes held until his phone made a noise. He silenced it and said with a groan, "I have to go get ready for work."

She followed him into the living room, which was empty, and only half of the floor was washed. By the door, he grabbed his coat. "Are you going to be okay tonight? You can sleep at my house if it helps."

"I'm okay. I'll stay at Evie's." She had forgotten he would not be at his house tonight.

"No going for a run in the middle of the night, then. Promise?" He brushed her cheek with his thumb.

"I won't," she agreed, not bothering to hide the smile pulling at her lips.

"Call me if you need to. I'll have my phone on me." He kissed her firmly on the mouth and left. Zoey watched his pickup as it drove down her driveway and towards his house. Once he was gone, she couldn't help but think, *Now what do I do?*

With a stiff resolve, she decided she could sleep without him. Shutting off the lights on her newly installed floors, she headed out to her truck and drove the short distance to Evie's house. Zoey sat in the truck for a moment, trying to get the courage up to go into the house and face an angry Evie, but when she got into the house, she only found a note on the table saying that Evie and Ben went to town for supper.

Sighing, she went straight to her bedroom and shut the door. Tomorrow would be soon enough to deal with Evie, but she knew tomorrow might be a long way away with Gabe working all night.

CHAPTER 22

IT TOOK two days before the tension got high enough between the sisters for them both to blow up. Zoey had been walking on eggshells around her older sister, but nothing she did was right or good enough. It didn't help that Zoey hadn't had more than an hour of sleep in two days, and her old constant state of exhaustion was back. Maybe it was the tension that was keeping her from sleeping this time, and not the fear of a nightmare. She had talked to Gabe a few times, but not enough to calm her rising temper.

Trying to get everything done perfectly like her sister wanted had been a difficult task because Zoey got in the way of perfection, as usual. She had been charged with moving the pigs to a new pasture, but had ended up forgetting the gate was open and spent over an hour chasing wiggly pink pigs around the yard. Then she had realized that while they were out, they had nearly destroyed the only large garden in her yard. Evie caught her trying to replant the little growths before they died.

"What happened?" Evie questioned, coming upon Zoey in her task. Her tone stated there was no explaining away what had happened.

"Pigs," was all Zoey could say, trying not to cry. She willed herself not to cry. Not today. Not in front of Evie!

"You let the pigs out?" Evie demanded, as if Zoey would do it on purpose. Like she had no business doing just the simplest tasks.

"No… Yes… I forgot to shut the gate," Zoey admitted, still trying to replant the little plants.

"So, this garden is destroyed?" Evie's tone was calmer than Zoey had expected.

Zoey kept working feverishly. "No, I can fix it. I just have to get the plants back in the ground."

"It doesn't work that way, Zoey. All these plants are gone, dead." Evie plucked one from the ground and threw it on the lawn beside her. "No pumpkins this year."

"I'm fixing it," Zoey insisted, still staring at the ground.

"There is no *fixing* it. Once the roots are out of the ground, you cannot put them back in." Evie stood on the other side of the flower bed, yelling now.

Flinching, Zoey wondered if her sister meant her. Was she saying that since Zoey had left, there was no coming back? That Evie wanted her to leave?

Zoey looked up and over at Evie. "We can buy started pumpkins in town. This time, we can plant them out in the field and not in this tiny garden. Put in a few acres of them." She pointed to the field where tiny corn plants were showing up in straight lines.

"There's corn out there," Evie said, deadpan.

"We can cultivate the corn and plant the pumpkins. More of them, too. We could have a pumpkin patch and have people come out and pick pumpkins in the fall!" Zoey had been thinking about this for weeks. It would bring money to the farm without hauling hundreds of pumpkins to town.

"Not going to work. We have to replant in the garden," Evie replied flatly, using her 'no argument' tone. Zoey's ideas weren't worth Evie's time.

"It would work! I can cultivate the corn while you go to town to get pumpkin plants." Zoey wasn't letting go of her idea. She had been thinking about it for weeks—it was a good idea.

"It won't work, Zoey. We will do it the same as before; we can't change now." Evie was starting to get angry.

"Evie, it might work. Can't we go with my plan for once? Just this once?" Zoey stood up to face her sister, taking her stand.

"No." Shaking her head, Evie picked up another dying pumpkin plant and tossed it on the lawn.

"Yes. One small change," Zoey shot back.

Evie looked into her eyes. "No change."

"Why not?" Zoey held her gaze, folding her arms over her chest.

"Because you won't be here in the fall, and I'll have to pick all those pumpkins myself. I have been doing this all by myself for years now, and I can't have you adding more work to my list. I barely get everything done as it is!" Evie admitted what Zoey had feared she had been thinking.

"I'll be here." Zoey shot back; her throat felt tight. Was Evie going to tell her to leave?

"No, you won't. You'll find something you want to do more. Who knows what Zoey's going to do with her life?" Evie kicked at a pumpkin plant in the garden, sending a spray of dirt into the air.

"I want to *farm*!" Zoey shot back.

"Since when?" Evie demanded.

"Since high school, Evie! Before Dad made me join the Army, I wanted to stay here and farm with you guys." Zoey finally admitted her secret to her sister. "I always wanted to farm with you and dad."

"Why did you join the Army and stay in it so long if you always wanted to farm so bad?" Evie put her hands on her hips.

"Because Chief Martin and Dad decided the Army would knock some of the *crazy* out of me. I joined because Dad was *tired* of me and couldn't even look at me after the fire. I stayed in because you didn't want me here, before or after Dad died." Zoey fought the tears threatening her eyes.

"I wanted you here, but you were out of control. We didn't know what to do with you." Evie threw her arms in the air.

"How would you have acted if you had to live with a man who hated you and resented the fact that he had to raise you?" Zoey wiped a tear with her dirty hand.

"He didn't hate you, Zoey, he loved you. He loved us all and loved raising us." Evie defended her father.

"Of course, he loved you and Della; you were his favorites. But me? No, he hated me more and more every year. I spent four years alone with him in that house; you didn't." Zoey pointed at the house behind her sister as another tear rolled down her face.

"I lived right over there. I worked with the man every day, and he had no idea what to do with you. He thought you would get pregnant like me and was scared stiff about it." Evie threw back at her, eyes angry.

"Then he would never be rid of me, right? Then he would have to help raise another bastard in his house," Zoey yelled.

"What does *that* mean?" Evie marched over the dirt to stand closer to Zoey. Ben had been conceived before Evie had been married.

"Didn't he ever tell his favorite daughter? Didn't he tell you the truth?" Zoey smirked up at her taller, older sister.

"Tell me what?" Evie countered. She was visibly shaking with rage at this point.

"That I'm not Charley's daughter. He was stuck raising Mom's bastard." Her voice didn't shake as she said the words that had changed her life so many years before.

"Liar, you're as much his as I am." Evie defended the truth as she saw it.

"Brown," Zoey pointed to her eyes. "Nobody has brown eyes, Evie, just me."

"That means nothing!" Evie countered, waving a hand dismissively.

"We did blood tests in our tenth-grade science class. It would be impossible for him to be my father with my blood type. I am not his." Zoey said, chin up.

"But then he loved you enough to raise you when he didn't have to," Evie countered.

"He only raised me because he couldn't find the other man and give me back. She left me with him when she walked out. He had no choice but to raise me." Zoey felt another tear fall from her eye.

"He loved you, no matter who your dad was. Our dad loved you. He loved getting letters from you after you left. They were always on the table at his house, and he would read them over and over again.

He would tell anyone who would listen about his daughter in the Army and what great things you were doing over there. He waited for you to come home so he could apologize, but you never did." Evie was crying as she said the words.

Tears were running freely down Zoey's face as well. "He never came to visit me when I was stateside! I was gone for years, and he never tried to visit me. Not once. When I came home from Afghanistan the first time, I wanted him to be at the airport when I got off the plane, but he didn't come. I asked him to come, and he still didn't."

"He was sick, Zoey. He'd had a small heart attack and couldn't go —you know that. He couldn't fly, and you were landing in New York." Evie said the same thing she had said years before when it happened.

Zoey looked at the sky, trying to fight back her tears. Barely audible, she added, "You never came either! I wanted someone there. Someone to welcome me home, but nobody ever came."

"You're right. I was too wrapped up in my life. I had a kid and a dead husband. I was young, but I should have been there. Every time you got off a plane, I should have been there." Evie tried to pull Zoey into her arms for a hug.

Zoey pushed her arms aside and turned to walk away, but stopped and said, "You keep saying you want the old Zoey back, but she died a little every time I stood alone in an airport with nobody to love me enough to be there when I came home. She died a little every holiday she spent alone, waiting for a call that never came, and a little more when she was discharged and had nowhere to go but to a home where she was told she wasn't good enough—that she wasn't wanted." Turning on her heel, Zoey walked away from her crying sister. Tears blurred her own vision as she went, but as long as she walked towards the large white blob, she would make to the house.

Zoey hadn't reached her destination before she heard Evie's truck roar to life and gunned out of the yard. She walked past the front door, and after she wiped her face with her shirt, she found her favorite spot from her childhood. Since she was small, whenever she would fight with her sisters or dad, she would sit and hide in the corner where the house met the back deck. She could see out from the little corner, but usually, nobody could find her. Sometimes, they hadn't even bothered to look.

Staring out at the field behind the house, she needed to regroup. Watching the tiny corn stocks blow in the wind in the distance, she wished she hadn't told Evie about her dad. Evie's relationship with him had been the envy of Zoey's high school years. She had always wanted to be as close to him as Evie was; even Della wasn't as close to Dad as Evie.

She suddenly wished she hadn't unloaded about them not being there for her when she was in the Army. The truth was, she really hadn't pushed them to be involved. She had wanted them to be there, but she'd also got tired of being disappointed when they didn't come. In the end, her family not being there had hurt her more than Zoey had ever let on. It had made her feel alone in the world.

Zoey sat in her corner for a long time, letting tears flow over things that couldn't be changed. Maybe the future would be better, but Evie would probably kick her out, and since Charley wasn't her dad, she had no claim to the house she was leaning against. Would Gabe let her move in? It seemed a bit early for that. They had only slept together a few times and had never said anything about a future together.

She should just go back to Evie's and pack up her things. Maybe Della can put her up for a few days; give her time to figure out her future—a future that left out everything she had ever wanted. Instead, she stayed in her hiding place, hiding from the world around her.

Zoey heard a car in her driveway and thought maybe it was Gabe, but he was sleeping and had no idea she had fought with Evie. Not wanting to see anyone else, she stayed in her spot, resting her forehead on her tucked-up knees. She heard footsteps but knew no one would find her in her spot, content to stare at the corn blowing in the wind— until a pair of jeans and boots came into view.

Her head snapped up to see Gabe's face. "Evie said you'd be back here. She said you had a fight. A big one."

Sitting down, he put his arm around her and pulled her close. "She said to say she was sorry, and that she doesn't want you to go anywhere. She said you're her sister no matter what, and she loves you." He kissed her head as they both watched the little corns blow in the wind.

He continued, "Something about plowing corn, and she'll visit more often. She's very upset and said she knew you wouldn't listen to her, but that you would listen to me."

They sat for a long time, staring out into the field beyond. "Nice hiding space," he said.

"Thanks. I guess Evie remembered it," Zoey sniffed. Together, they sat for another few minutes until they heard the roar of a truck coming from Evie, then over to Zoey's house.

The truck turned off after rumbling to a stop. Zoey tensed; Evie was coming. But instead, she heard the shed door open, and the tractor that was kept there come to life. Zoey sat and waited for Evie to leave with the tractor, but she drove around the yard for what seemed like forever.

Evie eventually emerged into Zoey's view, driving the red tractor with a cultivator attached. Zoey curiously watched as Evie started to cultivate up the tiny corns she had spent hours planting a few weeks before.

Zoey jumped to her feet—*what is she doing*? Gabe followed, then pulled her back to kiss her lips as he ran his fingers through her curls. "Go talk to your sister. I have to go to work."

Zoey tentatively strolled out to the cornfield her sister was destroying. Wiping her face with her shirt, she stood on the edge of her lawn and waited for Evie to stop. When they were parallel, Evie finally stopped the tractor and got out and walked to her sister.

Stopping in front of her, the sisters looked at each other with matching blotchiness from their earlier tears, not saying anything. They'd each come to terms with the change that their fight had caused between them.

"Your plan is good, Zoey. I should listen to you more. Tomorrow, we'll buy as many pumpkins seedlings as we can find." Evie's voice was raspy as she said the words, her eyes looking at the plants she had already dug up.

"You don't have to do this. It's your farm, and it always has been,"

Zoey said, admitting the truth. "I have no say in it. I'll pack my stuff and leave."

Evie grabbed her and hugged her close. "No, you won't. We're partners—it just took me a little too long to realize it. You have as much say as I do; you've earned it. I have to stop treating you like you're a kid."

"I *am* a kid," Zoey replied. Evie grew up fast, and Zoey never needed to.

"You've done more in your life than I have. I've never even left this farm." Evie shook her head as she kept hugging her sister.

Zoey pointed in the direction of her place. "You moved over there."

"And you fought in a war—twice," Evie insisted. "And I only had to think about what I would do if I lost you, every day, both times. But now you're here and safe, and a farmer."

"I was fine," Zoey assured her, even if she hadn't been at the time.

"I should've done more for you then; I know that. I plan to make it up to you now." She pulled away from the hug finally and said, "Go get rid of your corn. Make a big enough space for a pumpkin patch." She pulled Zoey in for another quick hug and whispered, "I love you so much."

"Love you too, Evie." Zoey smiled back as she pulled away and went to cultivate up tiny corns. Hoping her idea didn't flop.

CHAPTER 23

AFTER THE BLOWUP WITH EVIE, Zoey didn't know how much tension would be left when she finally walked into the kitchen that evening after finishing in the field. Evie and Ben had eaten and were watching TV in the other room. Zoey took off her boots and looked at her dirty pants, figuring she should change them before she ate. When she got to her room and peeled them off, she decided maybe a shower would make her feel better.

Clean and warm, Zoey walked out of the bathroom and almost ran into Evie in the hallway. Her sister was silent for a moment before saying, "Supper's waiting for you downstairs."

"Okay, thanks." Zoey nodded, and Evie went down the stairs. Standing at the top of the stairs a moment later, she decided she needed a sweatshirt to go over the t-shirt and leggings she put on after her shower. *Enough stalling, Zoey* she sighed and went down to face Evie again.

In the kitchen, Evie was putting together a plate of spaghetti for her, so she grabbed a can of pop and sat at the table. Evie set the plate down in front of her before sitting across from her with a coffee cup in her hands.

"Are you heading out tonight?" Evie asked.

"No, I'm in for the night." Zoey ate a bite of the food in front of her.

"All night?" Evie bit out and then quickly help up her hands and said, "Sorry. None of my business."

"You asked him to help you today," Zoey reminded her sister of the afternoon.

"I didn't know how else to get you to talk to me. He seemed to be hanging around a little too much suddenly. When I asked if he would talk to you for me, he didn't hesitate," Evie explained with a shrug.

"Gabe's a nice guy. Not all men are assholes, Evie. Just the one *you* married." Zoey quipped, instantly regretting the barb. Evie's head dropped to stare at her coffee cup, all the fight draining out of her. "I was there too, Evie. I might have only been in high school, but I know an asshole when I see one."

Evie sighed. "I didn't think you knew. I tried to shield you from it."

"Well, he wasn't my biggest fan and liked to think he could punish me. He beat the shit out of me when I got Jason Jensen kicked off the football team with the beer in his locker. I hid it from you and dad... There was a lot going on that year." Zoey looked at her sister. It had been the year that Ben had been born.

"I didn't think he hit anyone but me." Evie didn't look up from her coffee.

"Don't act so special, Evie. He knocked around anyone he could." Zoey pushed the uneaten plate away from her. "Gabe isn't like that."

Evie finally looked up from her coffee, now that the conversation had turned from her relationship. "I don't like you sneaking out at night like you do."

"Fine. I'll leave earlier in the day, so it's not sneaking," Zoey leaned back in the chair and crossing her arms.

"That's not what I mean. You don't have to hide things from me. I know you're an adult, and I understand, but he is kind of old, isn't he?" Evie asked before taking a drink of coffee.

"Thirty-nine, I think. He was in the Marines for twenty years." Zoey sat up straight, hoping that Evie would concentrate on his former career instead of Gabe's age.

"Wow, Zoey," Evie shook her head. "You remember you're only twenty-six, right?"

Zoey rolled her eyes. Evie had touched a nerve. "I can do math too, Evie. But it doesn't matter how old he is; he's done a lot for me. I don't know how I would have made it this far without him." Zoey nodded before continuing. "You and he should get along better. You both have the same issues with me: too young and don't exercise at night. Harp, harp, harp from you two."

"I don't harp; I'm just concerned." Evie pursed her lips as she tapped the table with her fingers.

"Don't be, please." Zoey leaned forward and grabbed her sister's hands tight. "He knows what I'm going through, and he's helping with it."

"Can't I help you?" Evie asked, in concern.

"You're helping, too. You're helping a lot. I just need him," Zoey admitted, what she had figured out weeks before.

"What about the mom thing? He *literally* drove her away from us." Evie pulled her hands out of her grasp.

"Oh, come on! He just drove her to the bus station, and he was just a kid." Zoey explained what Gabe had said.

"Do you believe that?"

"Don't you think she would've found another way to get away from us? She would have left no matter who drove. She didn't want to be our mom anymore." Zoey hated saying it out loud, but it was true. The words hung heavy in the air between them.

"I just don't like him." Evie broke the silence, shaking her head.

"I do. So could you just be nice to him, okay?" Zoey implored, knowing that if Evie let down her guard, she would eventually like Gabe.

Evie smiled. "I think you like him a lot."

"I think I do, too," Zoey admitted, not daring to look at her sister, who might see how much Gabe meant to her.

"Were you mad when he showed up today?" Evie asked. Zoey's eyes shot up and looked into Evie's green ones at the question.

"No, he was who I needed to see."

Evie chuckled. "I watched you guys sitting there all cute."

"He has a way of calming me. He's pretty good at it." Zoey remembered how she'd felt the minute he had shown up.

"I saw him kiss you goodbye. It was pretty hot." Evie winked at her.

"If you think that was hot, you should be dating more." Zoey giggled.

"No, no, I'll let you get all hot and bothered. I do *not* need a man in my life right now." Evie put up her hands in self-defense.

"Maybe we should start looking for someone for you to get hot and bothered with." Zoey laughed again as she watched her sister get uncomfortable.

"Never going to happen, Zoey," Evie said as she got up from the table and went to watch TV in the living room with her son.

Getting up from the table, Zoey threw away the uneaten food. She wasn't hungry tonight. After putting the dishes in the sink, she peeked into the living room at Evie and Ben, watching TV. Her heart felt for her sister—Evie had been a widow for a decade now and had no interest in meeting someone new. Zoey knew she was lonely, even with Ben around. Maybe Gabe knew someone that would be good for Evie.

* * *

ALLEN HAD BEEN RIGHT. Somehow, the guys in the department had found out about Zoey and him. His entire night shift had been hell because of it. Most of his fellow cops had either given him the cold shoulder or were outright combative. Gabe lost count of how many times he had been "accidentally" run into as he walked to his desk during the week. It was as if every cop in the county was her protector, and they were determined to run him off. Eventually, he had let them get under his skin.

This week, he had barely called or texted her since her fight with Evie. He had found excuse after excuse to stay away.

Evie pounding on his door had woken him from a deep sleep. Gabe had been surprised to see that Hart sister standing on his front step. He could tell she didn't want to be there, and that she was desperate.

In tears, she told him that she had messed everything up with Zoey.

Something about pigs and corn and pumpkins that he didn't understand. As she cried, he had wanted to give her a comforting hug, but figured she would beat him up if he did. Even if he hadn't caught everything she was saying, he had heard her say that she thought Zoey was going to leave.

Until that moment, he hadn't even thought about the possibility of Zoey leaving. She had a job and was working so hard to fix up her dad's house to live in. Those words had sent him into a small panic, and he would have agreed to anything Evie asked of him to get her to stay.

As they walked to their respective vehicles, Evie told him where she thought Zoey would be. Gabe stopped her and said, "Evie, Zoey is happy here. She talks about how much fun farming with you is, and how she's always wanted to do this. Even when she was in Afghanistan, she read books about farming. She won't just leave."

Then they both headed to Zoey's house. His heart was beating wildly in his chest as he searched for her, hoping she hadn't already left. He had thanked God he found her where Evie had said she would be, but his heart broke to see her sitting against the house, hugging her knees to her chest with tears running down her cheeks. It was the same position she had been in after her nightmare. He suddenly hated the woman who had asked him to come over here for what she had done to his Zoey, but he was thankful that she had asked him to help her.

Sitting there, holding her as she cried, he said nothing—he knew Zoey just needed to let things out. When she had finally gotten up to talk to Evie, his relief was almost palpable. She was staying. If she had still wanted to leave, she would have headed to Evie's house, not went to talk to the woman herself.

Staying long enough to watch the sisters exchange a long hug, then a shorter one, he knew they would be okay. To this day, he did not know what the fight had really been about; pigs, maybe, but he now knew that when they both exploded in anger, the fallout was massive.

As he got in his truck to start his four-day weekend, he hoped that things would be back to normal when he got back to work. He was starting to wonder if he would ever enjoy his job again.

CHAPTER 24

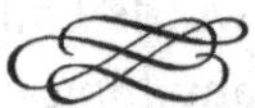

Zoey wished Gabe never had to go back to work. His four days off had
been amazing, and she had learned more about the man she was
falling more in love with every day. Gabe had come back to Birch Cove
to be closer to his mom after his dad had died. She was in a nursing
home, and he worried about how frail her health was. He told her
about his failed marriage and how he shouldered all the blame for it
not working out. She learned that he really didn't want to be a cop, but
it paid the bills, and he was qualified for it.

One rainy afternoon, Evie had let Zoey off work after lunch, and
she had been able to spend all afternoon with Gabe, watching it rain
from the couch in his living room. That was the day he had told her
about what had happened the two times he had been shot. Then he
talked about the buddies he had lost or nearly lost over there. She had
shared about her many experiences in the region and some other
things that kept her up at night.

Eventually, she had regaled him with stories from her misspent
youth, how she managed to always be in the middle of a situation
when it went south. She had him rolling with laughter about the party
senior year that started so innocently and ended with her in a jail cell.

Zoey loved that he had not judged her for things that happen back then, just excepted that she'd been out of control.

One day, she had even told him about her strained relationship with her dad. Gabe was silent as she explained how she had always felt different from her sisters. She knew that Evie and Della were four and six years older than her, which was a lot of years when you are a kid. But when she had completed the science experiment, and the result was glaring that Charley Hart could not have been her father, she had lost it. She had burned the assignment in the front yard, getting an F as a result, which involved getting detention. The small fire had actually caught into some dry grass and almost burned the barn down. The fire department had been called, so maybe that was why everyone was so unwilling to believe her about the school fire two years later.

But after that assignment, her relationship with Charley had not recovered. It spiraled for two years and culminated in her enlisting in the Army.

In purely Gabe fashion, he was able to tell her what she had not been able to see. Charley had truly loved her and had raised her as his own. Maybe he didn't even know. Zoey never brought it up with him, so who knew? Zoey and her sister Della were near carbon copies of each other, so why would he think one is his and not the other? He most likely had no idea how to harness the boundless energy of his youngest daughter and had no one to help him figure it out. Charley was probably more disappointed in himself as a parent than he was with her because he knew she was just a kid.

After Gabe had explained the other side, she wanted to talk to her dad more that day than she had since she was sixteen years old. At that point, she wanted him to hug her one more time and tell her he loved her. After crying like a baby in front of the man she loved, she had felt better about her past.

Gabe and Zoey had made love every chance they got. Gabe had helped her to get over the embarrassment she had felt when they made love by telling her that everything she did was amazing and perfect. By the third night of his mini-vacation, she had no insecurity around him—nothing but pure bliss.

On the morning of his first day back at work, she looked at the clock beside her head and cursed it a little. It was half-past four, and in an hour and a half, she would have to share him with the world. Rolling in his arms so she could look at his face, she was thankful that he had left the light on, but then again, he had always left the light on for her. Zoey found that she had been sleeping better now that the nightmares weren't coming as often. She had even been able to control her reaction to them, but she still was not ready to wake up in darkness. Maybe one day, but not yet.

Zoey fought the urge to touch Gabe's hair. The blonde locks were absolutely mouthwatering, sticking every which way. Zoey loved it when his hair was messed up; he seemed less in control that way. And she *really* loved it when he was out of control.

"You're awake." She watched his mouth say.

"I didn't want to wake you," she replied, smiling.

"You're staring at me…can't sleep through that. Too many years as a Marine." He rolled to face her. "What are your plans today?"

"Whatever Evie says to do. But she's started asking what I want to do, so maybe she's changing."

"She loves you and wants you happy, my Hart."

"Can I come over after you're done with work today?" She had never asked before, just shown up.

He pulled her closer to him. "Yes."

"Good." she smiled as she melted into his arms.

CHAPTER 25

GABE WAS STILL THINKING about that morning when Allen cornered him about the 'Zoey situation,' as Allen called it, pulling him into an empty office.

"Leave Zoey Hart alone, Gabe."

"What are you talking about?" Gabe played dumb.

"So, you're going to play it that way? Her new truck has been spotted at your place. *Overnight,*" Allen hissed.

"It's none of their business," Gabe countered.

"Gabe, she's half your age."

"No, she isn't. What does age have to do with it, anyway?" He asked, knowing it was his biggest argument about getting involved with her. Hearing it from another made it hard to argue it.

"She's a kid." Allen leaned against the table and stared at Gabe, judging him.

"She's twenty-six and has been in Afghanistan twice. She is a *woman.*" Gabe was starting to think these people still saw her as a troubled eighteen-year-old. A girl who needed protecting.

Allen leaned against the desk in the center of the room. "What are your intentions? Marriage?"

"Can't we just date or something?" Gabe didn't want to think about marriage. When Zoey got married, it would be to someone else. Marriage was for others, not him. Not them. Gabe rubbed his face with his hands to get the image out of his head.

"It's the 'something' that I'm not liking." Allen pursed his lips.

"It's not up to you to like it," Gabe reminded him.

"It's not just me who has an issue with it! No one out there is happy either." Allen pointed at the door they had walked in—at all his fellow cops.

"She's not the wild and crazy teenager you guys all think she still is. Zoey's learned to control most of that. Have any of you even seen or talked to her since she came back?" Gabe shot back. He had noticed that she never went to town, and when she did, it was just for a quick trip. As far as he knew, she hadn't even tried to reconnect with her former friends.

"No, she's stays at Evie's most of the time."

"Allen, I'm going to tell you something that you can go tell all those asses out there. War changes people, and she was over there…twice. Maybe you should stop being the protectors she *doesn't* need and try being the friends she does." Gabe walked to the door and opened it to leave.

Allen stood up and said, "She deserves better than you."

Gabe shot back as he left the room, slamming the door behind him. "I know."

He hadn't talked to Allen after that. In fact, he hadn't talked to anyone for the rest of his shift. All he had really done was sit at his desk and stew over what Allen had said.

Of course, Allen had been right—he was too old for Zoey. Once she started going out and seeing friends, she would realize he was just an old man. An old man who had fallen in love with a crazy, young redhead. Had he started falling for her that first night when she was in his arms in the middle of Main Street, or had it come later when she had held his hand all night to sleep? All he knew was that after he had spent the day working on flooring with the two sisters, he knew he was deeply in love with one of them.

But nobody who knew about their relationship approved of it.

From Evie to his fellow cops, everyone thought it was a bad match. Was he and Zoey wrong, and everyone else right? He didn't know.

He needed to stay away from her, he decided. Zoey needed to find someone her age. She had been so proud when she had told him she had slept alone when he was working, telling him she had even had a nightmare but had been able to handle it alone. Soon, she wouldn't need him anymore.

It was then that he saw her truck as he pulled into his driveway. His heart flipped in this chest as he watched her jump out of the red truck. She was wearing black leggings and a blue button-up shirt today. He wanted to slowly peel the entire outfit off her while running his fingers through her gorgeous hair.

"Gabe! Evie said I could leave a little early today. I hope that's okay." Meeting him as he opened his door, she tried to kiss him, but he pulled away, needing to keep the distance.

Pushing her away, he ignored her look of confusion as he walked into the house, trying to ignore the hurt in her eyes as she followed him. He knew he had to make this break before he couldn't do it anymore—before she fell for him. "Sorry, I didn't expect you to already be here," he said truthfully. He had needed a little time to get his heart ready for what he needed to do.

"I guess I am a little early…" He could hear the disappointment in her voice.

"Yeah, a little bit. I actually have to go back out and do something. I was just about to head back to town," he lied, unable to tear his eyes from hers. Confusion clouded the brown depths.

"Where are you going?" She questioned as she walked over to him, touching his chest with one hand.

"None of your business, Zoey." Gabe took a step back, forcing her hand to fall away, but the imprint of warmth remained on his chest.

"I thought we had plans tonight," she mumbled.

"I forgot. Sorry," he said, his mind chanting 'sorry… sorry… sorry…' over and over in his head.

"Okay, can I come over later, then? When you get home?" He could see the hurt in her eyes, and it was killing him.

He lied again. "I don't know if I'm coming home tonight."

The pain in her eyes was intense, then gone in an instant. Her back got straighter, and her chin went a little higher. "Are we done then?"

"It's for the best, Zoey." This time, it wasn't a lie. Gabe was glad to finally see her temper flare. Dealing with her anger was better than her pain.

"Can I ask why?" She demanded more than asked.

"You don't need me, and I sure don't need you."

She backed up as if he had actually slapped her with his words. Zoey closed her eyes for a brief moment, shaking her head. After she opened them again, she spun on her heels and stalked towards the door. Gabe started to follow, wanting to stop the pain he had caused her. He stopped himself before he could take a single step. It would be worse later if he tried to keep her—much worse. It was only a matter of time before she realized she didn't want him, anyway.

Stopping at the door, she opened it, then leaned her head against it as if the pain was too much. "I bought the bed. It's perfect." Then she was gone, slamming the door behind her.

Gabe made it to the door as he heard her truck rumble to life and take off down the road. He leaned against the door and said to the empty room, "I love you, Zoey Hart, but you deserve so much more than me. One day you will see that."

CHAPTER 26

ALL THE WALLS in Zoey's house had been painted a butter yellow in most rooms, except the first-floor bedroom was white. She had wanted the entire room to be white. Even though it was painful to think about, it was the only way she could see it.

The bed had arrived a week ago but was still sitting in boxes in Zoey's newly painted living room. All the other furniture that had arrived that day were now in place; the couch along the long wall in the living room, the table in the middle of the kitchen, and the counter stools were under the bar.

Now all she just had to put together the bed, and she would be able to live here, but she still couldn't open the box. It was a beautiful wrought iron bed and had cost more than Zoey had wanted to spend, but when she saw it in the store, she knew it was the bed she wanted to share with Gabe. That was before he stopped wanting her, though. Now he didn't want anything to do with her, and so far, she hadn't seen him. But every time she saw that bed, he was in the room with her, surrounding her…still loving her.

She forced herself to go back to unboxing new items for her kitchen. There was a giant box of cookware to open and silverware and plates. There were even glasses to put away, but Zoey didn't have the energy to do any of it. Her heart wasn't in her new house and all its new things anymore.

Evie walked in with a bag of stuff they had picked up the day before with Della in Minneapolis. Setting the bag down, she walked up to Zoey and hugged her. They hadn't talked about what happened at Gabe's house that day, but Evie understood anyway. Every time Zoey started down the pity path, Evie worked to get her beyond it.

"So, where do you want everything?" Evie asked, scanning the room still piled with boxes and bags of new stuff needing to be put away.

"Anywhere," Zoey said half-heartedly.

"We can do this another day, you know."

"No, I want to get out of your hair. You and Ben have been great to me, but you need to get back to being you two." Zoey picked up the box of silverware and went to the countertop to open it.

Evie grabbed something off the counter. "Who's this?" She asked as she looked at the picture.

Zoey glanced at the picture Gabe had found what seemed like a lifetime ago. "Gabe found it in the closet when he was putting in the floor." Zoey said his name and hadn't cried. It was a start, she realized. One small start.

"She looks like you, but the eyes are wrong." Picking up the picture, Evie analyzed it closer.

"Gabe thought she was Dad's love child. I told him Dad would never mess with another redhead after Mom." Zoey laughed a little.

Evie laughed at the suggestion as well. "Maybe it's Mom's love child."

"And she sent the picture to Dad? For what reason?" Zoey shook her head.

"I thought maybe it was a cousin."

"On Mom's side? She had no cousins, and the Connors were not that prolific until Mom came along. Though she looks a lot like you and Della," Evie mused.

"I guess we'll never know who she is." Zoey took the picture and hung it on the fridge door with the only magnet that was there. Pulling the tape off the box, she put the silverware into the tray Evie had brought over. The sisters worked at opening boxes and putting things in Zoey's new home for a few more hours, working mostly in silence.

Zoey was opening yet another box when Evie questioned gently, "Do you want me to put the bed together?"

Zoey couldn't respond because the tears were too close to the surface. "Zoey, can I?" Evie asked again.

"No," Zoey whispered to herself, then answered louder. "Yes, go ahead." She heard Evie moving around the living room and bedroom as she continued to work in the kitchen without turning around. Her heart wasn't ready.

Zoey threw the last of the boxes of kitchen items out the back door to be dealt with later when Evie came into the kitchen and said, "Okay, it's finished. It was easier than I thought it would be, so I made it also. Do you think you're ready to put away your clothes yet?"

"Tomorrow. I'll get groceries and bring my other stuff over then." Zoey pushed it off another day, needing another day.

"The bedroom looks great! Did you want to see it?" Evie walked past Zoey and ran her hand lightly over her hair.

"No," Zoey said firmly.

"Okay. Did you want to bring your entire room over here tomorrow, then? Bed and all, so Ben has somewhere to stay when he comes?" Evie said, as if it was normal for someone not to want to go into a room of their new house.

Zoey fought back the tears that were forming in her eyes. "Yes."

Evie gathered her in her arms and said, "That's what we will do, then. We'll make Ben a room."

Zoey nodded. "Ben's room." Both sisters knew the eleven-year-old would not be spending many nights in a bedroom a quarter-mile from his own. "Thank you for helping me, Evie."

"That's what sisters do. They're there for each other, through good times and bad. I don't want to let you down again," Evie said, gently pushing her sister away before adding, "I'll head home to make supper. Come when you're ready."

Zoey smiled at her sister. "Okay."

Hearing Evie's truck leave the yard made Zoey feel completely alone. She should be ecstatic to be alone in her own home, but it only felt overwhelming. Could she handle her own home? She couldn't even handle her own emotions anymore.

Scanning the surrounding rooms, she loved how everything had turned out—comfy furniture and calming colors everywhere. Her eyes caught on the open doorway to the bedroom. She hadn't been in there since the day she and Gabe had made love on the floor. Evie had painted the walls for her, and now she had put up the bed to where Zoey could see the end of it, complete with a folded fluffy white blanket. With all her courage, she walked over to the room and peered in. It looked just like she had wanted it to; just as Gabe had told her it would look…minus him. Minus his love.

Reaching out, she grabbed the doorknob and slammed it shut. She'd deal with it later, she decided. *Much* later.

* * *

GABE DIDN'T WANT to drive by Zoey's and Evie's house every day, but somehow, he managed to do it more than once a day. Whether it was when he was working or when he was off, every road led past the two houses.

Many nights, it was around midnight that his body propelled him to stop tossing and turning and just drive by to make sure the light was on in her room. He wanted to make sure that she was there and safe, not running in the dark night. Then, late last week, he noticed a light on in the middle of the night was on in Zoey's house and not in Evie's house anymore. Had she finally getting her dream of having her own place? He wondered if she was excited, and wanted to call her and talk about it, but didn't.

After that night, he only had eyes for the new house to see which lights she had on. Mostly, all the lights were on, but sometimes, it was only the kitchen light or the living room. But no matter what light was on, he tried to peer into the windows to catch a glimpse of her, but never did.

What he had done was the best thing for her, but it was pretty much killing him. He wasn't sleeping anymore, and work was dragging him down. Most of the guys had lightened up a little, but some were still being jerks. But they were nothing compared to the voices in his head, reminding him she deserved better.

The Birch Cove Farmers Market had just started for the season, and he caught a glimpse of Zoey and Evie selling their vegetables and jellies. It took everything in him not to go over there and talk to her, just to hear her voice again. Maybe she would laugh for him. She had looked great, and he had watched for a few minutes as she talked to a young man her age. Maybe they would start dating and get married, and his heart would be crushed even more than it was today.

The pain he had felt as he watched the couple talk over jellies and jams made his divorce seem like a walk in the park. When his ex-wife had introduced him to her new husband, he had been nothing but happy for them. His ex-wife had deserved to be happy, but seeing Zoey with a strange man interested was a punch in the gut. A punch he deserved for pushing her away. Maybe he should have just waited until she was done with him since the pain would've been the same, but at least he would have had a little more happiness before this despair.

Evie had caught sight of him watching Zoey, and she had started walking towards him, but he turned and left the gathering. He didn't need Evie telling him to stay away from her sister—he was already trying his hardest to do that, and look where that had left him.

Her hat was still sitting on the dash of his pickup, reminding him of her every time he got in. He was going to leave it in her mailbox one day, but his hand couldn't pick it up from his dash, so he had simply driven away. At least he had something of hers.

CHAPTER 27

THE PUMPKIN PATCH had become Zoey's project, and she worked in her little pumpkin patch every day. Every morning, she would look out her kitchen window to see if they had grown for her, and they usually did. Using the little plants as an excuse to be alone had worked; Evie didn't bother her when she was in her pumpkin patch.

The little plants didn't diminish the emptiness in her heart, but they made her happy. In the month since she had last seen Gabe, her life had changed. The house was done, and she was living in it full time. She slept in her old bedroom upstairs in the bed they had brought over for Ben to sleep in, but at least she was sleeping in her own house. So far, she still hadn't opened the downstairs bedroom door. A few days ago, she had decided that once she was able to open the door, she would take out the bed and replace it with a different bed completely. One that had no connection to Gabe Watson.

Evie had really taken the training wheels off on the farm. Zoey could now decide what she wanted to do and when. Every morning, they discussed what needed to be done, and each was able to decide what they wanted to do for the day.

Farmers Market season had started, so now every Friday night and

Saturday afternoon were busy in Birch Cove and Minneapolis. They usually met up with Della in the city for coffee or lunch on those trips. Neither had brought up Gabe, but Zoey could see that they both wanted to. Della had filled them in on the end of her relationship with the guy from her office. Della wasn't as devastated about its end as Zoey was about hers.

Ben was now out of school, and he and the little neighbor girl were the farm's summer employees, bringing some much-needed talk and laughter to the gardens. Clementine Reed lived next door with her grandparents, who needed the twelve-year-old girl out of the house and busy for the summer. Since she was one of Ben's best friends, she was welcomed and put to work.

Life was good, except for the emptiness that Gabe had left in her life. At the Farmers Market, she had been asked out by three different men, but none of them were Gabe, so she turned them down. Maybe one day, she would be ready to date, just not yet.

Since the markets had started, she had talked to quite a number of the cops that used to take her home after her adventures as a crazy youth. They had seemed disappointed that she wasn't the crazy kid they used to know anymore. Zoey almost wanted to apologize to them for growing up, but she didn't, because she wasn't.

Since the pumpkins in her back yard were her idea, she made them her responsibility. Zoey wanted to show Evie that her plan for these babies was a great one and that they were not going to be something else Evie had to do. As she hoed them, she was wearing shorts, a tank top, and her usual hat in the heat of the day. *I should put on more sunscreen*, she thought, *redheads don't tan well.*

Walking towards the house, she watched as Evie's truck made the circle from her yard to Zoey's. Though the corn was growing, and she would soon not be able to watch her sister's movements in her yard, today she saw the entire progress. Shifting her route, she headed to meet her in the driveway. Evie pulled to a stop and rolled down her window as Zoey got closer to the truck. "Get packed!"

Zoey blinked, not understanding the comment. "What?"

Evie was grinning. "Get packed, Zoey."

"Why?" Zoey questioned.

"Della's taking you to Vegas!" Evie couldn't hide the excitement in her voice.

"*Las Vegas*?" Zoey's jaw dropped in surprise; she had no idea what was going on.

"There's only one Vegas, Zoey." Evie laughed at her expression.

"Why?"

"You only turn twenty-seven once, and Della wants to take you to Vegas." Evie opened the truck door and hopped out. "Let's get you packed."

"I don't think I want to go to Vegas, Evie," Zoey argued. She had her pumpkins to take care of.

Pulling a carry-on suitcase out of the back of her truck, Evie started for the house. "Too bad. Tickets are already purchased, and you guys leave tonight. You have to be at the airport by six."

"But—"

"No buts! I'm tired of seeing you moping around here. I need a few days away from it," Evie said as she went into the house.

"Really?" Zoey asked. She had thought she had hidden her sadness better than that.

"No, but you need some time away from here. You've been working harder than me these last few weeks. I have the kids to help me, so we'll be okay," Evie explained.

"There are too many people in Vegas," Zoey tried to back out again, but she knew Evie didn't understand her issues with crowds.

"Della said the airport isn't as busy if you take later flights, and she has the perfect hotel picked out." Evie tried to calm her sister's nerves. "You have been doing really good at the farmer's markets, and there's a lot of people there."

"Why aren't you going with?" Zoey asked as she watched her sister pack her suitcase for her. Why stop her if she was doing it already? This way, Zoey didn't need to do the task.

"We can't both be gone at the same time in the summer," Evie explained with a head shake, as if Zoey should have known that already. Zoey was convinced Evie was making up the rules as they went along, but wasn't going to argue.

"I guess I have to go then." Zoey watched Evie close the suitcase.

"I hope you can fake excitement better for Della, Zoey. She's paying for this little adventure." Evie left the room and Zoey behind. Zoey looked around and grabbed a few things Evie hadn't packed, then scrambled down the stairs after her.

When she got to the bottom of the stairs, Evie turned to her and said, "You have to change. Go put on something nice."

Zoey looked down—had she really not even thought of changing out of the faded cut-offs and red tank top she was wearing? Laughing, she went back to her room and changed, realizing she hadn't laughed in days.

When she came back down the stairs in blue shorts and a cream-colored top, she found Evie was outside, putting the small carry-on in Zoey's truck. The sisters hugged, and Zoey climbed in the truck, wondering why she was letting her sisters bully her into a trip. But she knew it would be better to spend some time away, even if she didn't want to.

Almost turning around a hundred times during the two-hour drive, but knew she would disappoint both her sisters and waste Della's money if she chickened out. Evie had left her printed ticket on the passenger seat and said Della would meet her there.

After she had checked in, she stood waiting for her sister. A sudden thought popped into her mind: *What if Gabe is the one I'm going on this trip with?* What if he had planned this whole thing to get her back? She started looking around the airport for the man she loved, the man she missed so much. One time she thought she'd actually seen him walking towards her, but as the man got closer, she saw it wasn't him. Her heart was actually breaking again with the disappointment.

Zoey made herself stop looking around and tried focusing on her phone instead. Hoping it would take her mind off him. Except she needed more than a few minutes of mindless activity for that.

It wasn't working too well, but she finally stopped watching for him when she spotted her sister rushing her way, a carry-on in hand. Zoey let go of the Gabe dream and got up to hug her oldest sister. Maybe they would get rid of Della's brown locks in Vegas. Maybe she would be able to get Gabe out of her heart in Vegas as well.

* * *

GABE HAD BEEN worried sick about Zoey last night when he had driven by her house and found all the lights off. Had something happened to her? He wanted to pull in, but it was after midnight, so he didn't want to wake her if she was actually sleeping. So Gabe had gone home and tossed and turned for a few hours before sleep finally came. His alarm woke him way too early, and he had another bad day at work.

Most of his fellow cops had stopped acting like jerks, and there were only two that kept it up at this point. Both were just holding the grudge because they could, not because they had any feelings for Zoey.

Finally, he had a few days off and had a lot of yard work ahead of him—anything to keep his mind off redheads. 'Keep busy' was his new motto.

When he turned into his drive, his heart started beating a little faster when he saw a familiar truck sitting by his house. Zoey was okay. He breathed a sigh of relief until he saw a blonde sitting in the driver's seat. Evie was definitely not the sister he wanted to see.

He took a deep breath and climbed out of his truck while Evie climbed out of hers. As she walked his way, Gabe noticed how much she moved like her sister, and he missed Zoey even more. "Hey, Evie."

"Watson." Evie's unsmiling voice was clipped and all business; her attitude towards him hadn't changed since he had last seen her either.

"Gabe," he corrected her.

"Gabe, I guess," she said through her teeth.

"Is Zoey okay?" He had to know—her light had been off.

"Yeah. As good as she could be since you dumped her." Evie leaned against the front of her truck, refusing to look at him.

He leaned against his truck the same as her and looked out at the same field she looked at. "I didn't dump her; I ended it before emotions got involved."

"So, your emotions weren't affected?" Evie demanded.

"No," he lied.

"So, you drive by her place every day just *because*? It's miles out of the way."

Damn, Evie had seen him. He just hoped it had been once and not every day.

"I, um… I," he had no answer.

"I see you, but I don't think she does. I saw you at the Farmer's Market also," Evie stated.

"I just want to make sure she's okay." He folded his arms over his chest. Did he really have to defend himself to Evie? She hadn't wanted him anywhere near her sister, so why was she annoyed when he was finally staying away from her?

"She was, then you stomped her into the dirt. I have no idea what you said, but it nearly destroyed her." Evie said, and Gabe's heart broke a little at the news; Zoey had looked like she was getting over him.

"She looks good when I see her," he countered.

"You mean at the farmer's market? She wears makeup and puts on a happy face. Most of the time, she looks just as crappy as you do." Evie sneered and crossed her arms as she looked at the grass beyond them.

"She's better off without me, Evie. She deserves someone her own age—we both know that," he murmured, digging the toe of his boot into the ground a little.

"Do we? I really don't care how old the person is who can make my sisters happy. The most important part is their happiness. She was happy with you, and you took that away from her. Were you ever happy with her?" Evie finally looked at him.

"Very," he admitted with a nod.

"Then maybe if you stopped listening to your brain and just started listening to your heart, you could both be happy again. Happiness isn't something that you have your entire life, so when you find it, you have to grab it and hold on. Then, live life knowing it could be gone tomorrow." Evie's eyes drifted back to the field in front of them.

"Wise words, Evie."

"Also, remember that Hart's are very stubborn people. You dumped her, so she isn't going to come back to you. You have to go to her." Pushing away from her truck, Evie walked to her truck door and opened it before adding, "She's in Vegas with Della today. It's her birthday. She'll be back in two days if you care."

Lost in thought about missing her birthday, he heard her drive out of the yard, but he didn't turn to watch her go. Gabe's mind was too busy churning over the things she had told him. She had basically given him the rough plan on getting Zoey back, though she didn't even want him in her sister's life. Now, he had two days to figure out if she was right about the arguments that had been floating in his head. He couldn't live without her, and maybe she felt the same way.

Could it be possible that she fell for him just as hard as he fell for her? That all the excuses he had to keep them apart were just that —excuses?

CHAPTER 28

THE BIRTHDAY TRIP had gone better than Zoey had thought it would. She had expected to be dragged all over the city to gamble or go to shows, but Della hadn't made any plans, so they just did things they thought would be fun. Zoey smiled at how different her older sisters were.

They had spent the first night at the hotel, just talking. Zoey had actually told her a little about what had happened with Gabe, and Della had told her about her now-ended relationship with the guy from work. Zoey was a little concerned that her sister's relationship was in a worse place than Zoey's, and Zoey's was over. Della didn't seem too concerned about it at all.

When night came, Della had said nothing when Zoey had left the bathroom light on and the door wide open. Della accepted that it was what Zoey needed, and oddly, Zoey had been able to sleep with her sister in the room. Deep down, she must've felt safe enough with her older sister to let her guard down. Happily, the nightmares stayed at bay the entire trip.

The next day, they had gone out for makeovers. Zoey had gotten her hair cut and styled, and Della had gotten her dark brown hair colored to a softer brown, nixing Zoey's idea of going back to red. How many times Zoey had heard 'lawyers don't have red hair' that day, she didn't know. They had also splurged on mani-pedis, and Zoey smiled when Della picked out a bright "redhead" color for her nails.

They had some wine during the makeover and with lunch—maybe too much, because afterwards, Della had decided that the sisters needed to get matching tattoos. The wine must have dulled Zoey's defenses because soon they were a few blocks from their hotel, sitting side by side in a tattoo parlor.

Zoey's chosen spot was on her hip, and her tattoo was a heart about the size of a quarter. It had been more painful than Zoey had expected it to be, but she had fought through it to the finish. Della, meanwhile, had hers put down her side near her bra line, but it was bigger. Hers composed of three hearts, one for each sister. Two were filled in red, and one was just a red outline. Zoey couldn't believe her strait-laced lawyer sister was actually in a tattoo parlor, let alone getting a tattoo. But then again, Zoey had been noticing she wasn't the only one with a wild streak in her in the family.

They were so happy with the new ink that they kept showing strangers. Maybe too much wine *had* been consumed, but after the tattoos, they had gone out to celebrate Zoey's birthday and had more alcohol over supper. They had even taken some back to their room when the crowds got to be too much for Zoey.

The following morning, Zoey had sworn off booze forever. Apparently, she liked to drunk text, all of which were sent to Gabe. Most were of her cleavage—her very unimpressive cleavage. One was just the word 'jerk.' So, this morning, she had also sent a sorry text, hoping that he didn't think anything of it. She had sworn to leave him alone and had achieved her goal until yesterday. Today, she started anew with leaving him alone... and added leaving alcohol alone to the list as well.

At the end of the trip, the two sisters let the plane empty out in Minneapolis, just as they had in Las Vegas days earlier, before they grabbed their suitcases and headed off. Both were laughing and joking about something that had happened on their trip as they made their way through the airport when Zoey looked up and saw a sea of signs. They all said: Welcome home, Zoey! Tears stung her eyes. This was the homecoming she had always dreamed would happen. Evie was there with Ben, and their next-door neighbors, Grandma Betty, Grandpa Bill, and Clementine, were with her. They were all holding signs, but so were about forty other people Zoey had never seen before. Evie's sign was the only one that said something different. Hers said: Missed you!

Evie dropped her sign and ran to her, throwing her arms around Zoey. Della joined in, and her sisters hugged her tight. "I told you that you would never get off a plane again without me being there. I promised," Evie said as all three sisters cried in the middle of the airport, surrounded by all the signs that had always been missing from Zoey's trips home.

CHAPTER 29

Zoey couldn't help but smile on her way home from Minneapolis the next day; her sisters were amazing. When they had left the airport last night, Betty and Bill had taken the kids home to Birch Cove so the sisters could have a sleepover at Della's tiny apartment.

Before they made it to the apartment, Della had insisted Evie needed a matching tattoo as well, so, after an internet search and a few calls, she and Della were watching Evie get inked also. Not surprisingly, the middle sister was not as happy about it as the others had been. Zoey felt her sisters were trying too hard to cheer her up for her birthday, but she was loving watching her sisters let loose a little. Something she had been sure had not happened often enough for them.

Then they had gone back to Della's and talked. They had reminisced about growing up and all the things that they had done years ago, catching up on all the things that they had missed.

Della swirled her glass of wine, forgetting their morning hangovers. "Zoey, I wish I had forced Dad to let you move in with me that summer before you graduated."

"You couldn't have handled me," Zoey assured her sister. She had never known that Della had even thought about it.

"Oh, I could've handled you, but more importantly, you needed to get away from Dad. At the time, I convinced myself you were better off with Evie around than with me. She *is* the motherly one, after all," Della said with a smile.

"You're motherly, too, Della," Evie insisted.

"Why didn't you?" Zoey wanted to know.

"Because I would've had to talk to Dad, and I hadn't done that in years," Della admitted sheepishly.

"You came home all the time, though. I know you stayed with me, but you talked to Dad." Evie was still trying not to touch her new tattoo as she argued, confused by Della's reply.

"Nope. Nothing more than maybe 'hi, how's the weather.' We didn't have a relationship during the last ten years of his life. I came home to see you guys and Ben, of course." Della moved to fill her glass.

"I remember you talking to him, though," Evie insisted.

Della took a deep sip before answering. "You had a different dad than I did, Evie. Zoey had my dad. I just realized it was too late. I should have been there."

"There was nothing you could do, Della," Zoey assured her.

"I tried to get you out of the army. I talked to another lawyer about how to get you out, but you were already in basic training. You were eighteen, and I couldn't find a loophole to get you out. I've always felt bad about that," Della said.

"You did? You never said anything." Zoey's eyes widened slightly as she went to hug her oldest sister for trying for her all those years ago.

Hugging her tightly back, Della whispered, "But I failed! I couldn't get you out."

"It's okay, Della. In the end, I liked the Army. It took that to make me grew up and got the discipline I needed. I don't know what I would be like today if I hadn't enlisted… I needed it," Zoey admitted.

"No, it's not. I really messed up when I let him do what he did to you. I'm the oldest and should have seen it coming."

"You were working all hours of the day and night. I was there, and I let it happen. I didn't know how to stop it either," Evie chimed in, frowning at Della. Had she known what her sister had done? Or tried to do? Or had they never talked about it until now?

"Guys, seriously. It was my fault. I was out of control, and I can see that now. My life was crazy, and I needed what the Army gave me. Do I wish I had been here with you guys? Yes, of course! But I'm proud of what I've done, and I was a pretty good soldier." Zoey winked and offered a genuine smile.

"I bet you were. Della, she works harder than me now," Evie chuckled softly.

"I don't; Evie works the hardest. I just do what I can," Zoey said into her empty glass.

"Don't let her fool you. I'm lucky to have her as a partner." Evie smiled at her little sister.

Nobody said anything for a while, as all three were lost in their thoughts. This week had been more fun than Zoey had ever imagined. She had thought that she would spend the entire time thinking about Gabe. She had, to a point, but she had also let herself have fun with Della and Evie. Maybe, with both their help, she would be able to get over him. Or at least learn to live without him.

It was mid-afternoon when Zoey dropped Evie off at her house. As she grabbed her purse out of the cab, Evie had said not to come back today. She was going to take the rest of the day to rest, and so should Zoey. Zoey was more than happy to have a little time to herself. Her sisters had been great fun, but Zoey needed to unwind. Maybe she'd binge-watch something in her PJs.

But first, she had a project to do that she had been planning since she had gotten her tattoo. Zoey had decided that if she could endure the pain of getting a tattoo, she could take the bed apart in her bedroom. She just needed to take it down and put it in her spare room upstairs; then she could shut the door and leave it there until she knew what to do with it. It was a beautiful bed that didn't deserve to be thrown out. But it also couldn't stay in her bedroom.

Parking in front of her house a moment later, her face was a mask of determination. She grabbed her suitcase and took it upstairs, leaving it on the landing before her courage dissolved. Zoey quickly changed out of her jeans and into sweatpants before hurrying down the stairs again.

She headed down the stairs to the kitchen, where she dug in her junk drawer for a screwdriver. Zoey paused for a moment, smiling at the fact that she owned a junk drawer. She finally had the room in her life for junk that needed its own drawer.

Setting her jaw, she headed towards the closed door. She would always love Gabe, but his hold over her had to loosen, or she wasn't going to survive. And that would start with the bed and the memories it induced. Shaking her head, she remembered he had never even seen the bed, much less been in it. And neither would she. *What a waste,* she thought to herself.

Go, her head said, and she forced her feet to keep moving. Zoey grabbed the door handle, just as there was a knock on her front door. Was it a reprieve? Maybe she should just ignore the visitor and complete the mission. This needed to be done before she lost her courage and it was waning.

The knock came again, louder this time. Zoey threw her head back and groaned; the mission would have to wait. Still with the screwdriver in hand, she walked to the front door and swung it open, unable to stop the gasp that escaped her when she saw Gabe on her front porch.

She spun around and said, "No," nearly running to the kitchen. She left him standing on her front porch.

"Zoey, please stop. We have to talk," he implored, not moving from the doorway.

Zoey stopped but didn't turn around. "We have nothing to talk about; you said it all already. You don't want me."

"Zoey." The pain in his voice shocked her.

Closing her eyes, she let her head drop forward. "This is about the pictures I sent. I'm sorry—I was drinking, and you know how it is." She pulled her phone out of her pocket and held it out to her side so he could see it. She continued after a deep breath. "I'll delete you from my phone, so it won't happen again."

"Zoey," he said her name again, his voice quieter. He sounded sad, but she was not going to look at him. A second later, she heard the floor squeak as he came into the house.

Just breathe, Zoey, she said to herself. Zoey opened her phone and began scrolling through her contacts to find the name and number that Gabe had typed months ago. Her last connection with him. This was killing her. She had wanted to be able to see the words he had sent her for longer than this. She had memorized them over the past month, but after today, she would have only her memory.

She heard his footsteps coming up behind, and she panicked. "I'm deleting it, okay? I'm deleting it."

"Don't, Zoey," he said, sounding breathless. "Don't delete me, please."

She watched him reach over her shoulder and grab her phone. "That's mine!" Zoey turned and tried to grab the phone from his hand. Suddenly, she was face to face with him.

"Don't delete me from your life, Zoey." Gabe threw the phone onto the nearby couch.

Zoey watched it fly through the air and land softly against one of her new pillows. She was still looking at it when she spoke, not daring to look at him. "Please leave me alone, Gabe."

"Zoey, I lied to you." He was still too close.

She took a step back away from him, shaking her head. "I don't care anymore."

"I *do* need you, Zoey. I lied when I said I didn't before. Maybe you don't need me, but I need you."

"Gabe, stop." Her words were barely loud enough for her even to hear. She turned her back on him again.

"Damn it, Zoey, I love you," Gabe insisted, his voice a little more frantic. She could feel his hand on her shoulder. "I made the biggest mistake of my life when I tried to push you away. I started to believe the voices in my head that said you would never stay with me, that you deserved better than me, and that we should stop this affair before we fall in love. But I was already in love with you. You deserve someone far better than me, but I'm dying not being with you."

She turned back to him at his words. "I only want you. I've never felt like this about anyone before. I'm on an extreme high when we're together, and when you ended it, I fell into a hole I have yet to crawl out of. I could see the edge today for the first time, but the complete blackness showed up again when you did."

Gabe reached out and touched her wayward curl like he used to do. He said, "I don't want you to be in the dark, Zoey. I've spent our entire relationship bringing you out of that hole, and I've failed you. How can I help you back out?"

Zoey just shook her head. "I don't know, Gabe. I've never been so deep before."

Before she could walk away, he grabbed her into his arms and held her as tight as he could. Zoey suddenly felt his warmth encircle her, warming her for the first time since he sent her out of his life. Breathing his familiar scent, her body remembered him instantly and melted into his embrace. She had longed and dreamed of this for so long, but it didn't compare to the real thing.

Pulling her down with him onto the couch, he held her tight on his lap. They stayed that way for a long time, just holding each other. She felt him kiss the top of her head every once in a while, so lightly she wondered whether it had actually happened. Noticing she was still holding the screwdriver in her hand that he continued to hold. Zoey asked, "You said you were in love with me?"

He kissed her head harder, saying into her hair, "Completely, madly in love with you."

"When? When did you fall in love with me?" She asked quietly. She needed him to tell her.

"Looking back, I know I fell in love with your body and your spunk that night on Main Street outside Lobo. I had never been so instantly attracted to a woman before in my life. I had you in my arms, and I never wanted to let you go."

"What would have happened if I had said yes to a police escort home?" A slight smile pulled at her lips.

"Well, I probably would've been fired because I wouldn't have been able to keep my hands off you." Gabe was resting his head on hers, and she could feel him smiling as well.

"Why didn't you ever make any moves on me at your house? You just let me sleep with you."

"Because by the time you had shown up at my door, I knew enough about you to know you were there to heal. You needed healing more than sex. It wasn't as easy as I let you think it was, though. Seeing you wearing my shirt and nothing else drove me *crazy*."

"Good. At least I wasn't alone then." She wiggled to try to get even closer to him.

"I won't ever let you be alone again," he admitted, running a hand up her back.

"If you were so hot for me, why did I have to make the first move?" She leaned back and looked up at him in question.

"Because I was trying to be a gentleman, but sometimes slipped up and kissed you. I wasn't exactly sure how you felt about me, and I didn't want to give you mixed signals." He kissed her forehead again.

Zoey laughed. "They weren't mixed. I wanted into your pants outside Lobo, too. It took a moment, but I finally got my courage up to take advantage of you."

"You didn't take advantage of me. Is that why you had to go so fast that first time? Courage?"

"Yep. I had to get the first time out of the way before I could over-analyze it. After the rape, I didn't know if I would want sex. Even after I realized I wanted you, I wasn't sure how I would feel in that moment. If I would be able to enjoy it." She looked away from him as she spoke.

He took her face into his hands and turned it so that they were looking into each other's eyes again. "Don't be ashamed of what you couldn't control. Never let that have control over you. You are stronger than what happened to you."

Zoey just nodded, trying to fight back the tears forming in her eyes. He somehow knew what she was thinking about herself.

"Did you enjoy it?" He asked as he kissed the tears from her eyes.

She curled back into his arms. "You know I did. I always enjoyed it."

"Me too."

"You got the house looking nice. It's very cozy." He looked around the house from his spot on the couch as if seeing her place for the first time.

"Thanks. It took longer than I had planned to move in."

"Why? You were so excited," he said, glancing at her before looking around the room again.

"You weren't here, but you were everywhere I looked," she whispered, with her head still on his chest.

"Zoey, I am so sorry. I've been such a jerk." He pulled her closer and held her tight. "I used to drive by Evie's house every night to make sure you were there. Then you moved over here last week. I was so happy you had finally got it done."

"You drove by? When?" She asked in surprise.

"Every day. Before work, after work, at night when I couldn't sleep. So, every night." He hesitated for a moment before adding, "I also went to the Farmer's Market just to see you."

"I never saw you."

"I didn't want you to. I just needed to see you in person."

"Did it help?"

"Not a bit. When I saw you, I just wanted more. It just made the pain worse." His grip tightened on her.

"I know that pain." Zoey shifted so that she could see his face.

His eyes pleaded with hers, "Can we put the pain behind us, Zoey?"

"I... I don't know. If you walk out the door. I don't know if I'll survive it again."

"I don't want to ever walk out that door again, my Hart. If you want me, I am yours. I'm going to spend the rest of my life making you fall in love with me again." He kissed her head and nuzzled into her neck.

She pulled away to look into his blue eyes. "It won't work, Gabe."

She saw the pain she had just caused him with her words, recognizing it. Slowly, she touched his face and said, "You can't make me fall in love with you, Gabe. The falling's done. I have loved you my entire life; I was just waiting to meet you."

A radiant smile spread over Gabe's face, and he grabbed her face between his hands and kissed her. "God, I love you, Zoey Hart."

"I love you too, Gabe." She kissed him back. "I love you too."

He pulled away from her mouth and rested his forehead against hers. "A lifetime, huh?"

She smiled. "Maybe not a *lifetime*, but I've never put the moves on a man whose name I didn't know. I knew then that you were different."

"Different?"

"I never wanted to be out of your arms from the first moment I was in them. I completely fell for you when you defied Evie to help with the floor. If you stay around, you'll have to put up with Evie not liking you."

"She told me you were home."

Zoey pulled away and looked at him. "Evie? My Evie?"

"She stopped by two days ago and told me you would be home from Vegas today, and to call if I wanted to know what time. She called after you dropped her off." He smiled and pulled on a curl.

"What did she say?"

"She said she didn't like me and thought I was too old for you, but then she said I made you happy, and she wanted you to be happy." He ran his thumb over her cheek.

"Evie's a secret romantic."

He nodded and kissed her lightly, then kissed her again. "Yes, she is." He deepened the kiss and shifted her on his lap so that she was straddling him. God, he felt so good against her body. She wanted to melt into him.

"Zoey, what are you poking me with?" He leaned back and reached between them, and she felt him take something from her hand. "What's this?"

"A screwdriver." She took it and threw it on the couch beside them and started to kiss his neck again.

His hand was back on her body when he asked, "What's the screwdriver for?"

Without lifting her head, she replied, "I was finally strong enough to take apart the bed."

He pulled her away from him again, raising an eyebrow. "Our bed?"

She nodded. "Evie put it together for me, but I haven't been able to even go into that room." She glanced at the shut door behind them. "I was going to get rid of it today."

"I'm glad I showed up when I did, then," his voice was husky as he said it.

In one motion, he got up from the couch, taking her with him. She wrapped her arms and legs around him as he walked across the room. Gabe opened the closed door as she nuzzled her face into his neck and enjoyed his arms around her. Zoey pulled a particularly naughty move, and she both felt and heard him groan as he took them into the room. She pulled her head from his neck and peeked around the white room. With him there, the room wasn't as sad as it had been before.

She felt him lay her gently on the white sheets that had been unused in a month. He kissed her while running his hands through her hair, then stood up and asked, "Can I make love to you on our bed?"

"Yes," breathlessly she watched as he started to take his clothes off. She sat up to get rid of her clothes as well.

"No, I'll do that, babe," he said as he slowly pushed down his boxers, shedding the last of his clothes. Zoey simply stared. Gabe had *definitely* been working out since she'd last seen him. He was absolutely naked, and his glorious body settled into the bed beside her. "I've been dreaming of doing this for ages." He smiled as he turned to face her.

"Gabe..." was all she said when he started to pull off her t-shirt. He smiled at Zoey, eyes growing dark as he stared at her breasts, then he started to suckle them, making her moan. After he had loved on her breasts, he pulled off her sweatpants and tossed them across the room. He grinned up at her and then turned his attention to her lower half. His eyes immediately flew back up to her face.

"You got a tattoo! Is it real?"

"Yep! Happy Birthday to me," she said as she watched him marvel over the small heart on her hip. Then she laughed and grabbed him, flipping him onto his back and holding him down with her body. He started chuckling with her until she took him into her hands and started stroking him. She watched his face as she touched him, and when he finally closed his eyes, she moved above him and took him fully into her body. Gabe's eyes flew open, and he started to sit up, but she pushed him down with her hands and started to move. "Happy birthday to me," she repeated with a smirk.

She gasped when he spun them around, and she found herself under him again. She let him have his way and succumbed to the pleasure he provided, going over the edge as he did.

Out of breath and deliriously happy, Zoey laid on top of Gabe's chest. This was how she wanted to spend her life. "My soul knew you before I ever met you. It knew safety was in your arms. My mind and heart took some time to catch up, but my soul knew who you were once our eyes met. I couldn't get you out of my mind after that."

He played with her curls. "Evie isn't the only romantic in the family."

"I'm so glad I got into a fight that night at Lobo."

"I would have met you, anyway. Might have been easier without the fight."

"Easier, but not as good of a story for our grandchildren. Do you even think they'll believe it?" Zoey giggled.

"I didn't know there would be children, much less grandchildren."

"Oh, there's going to be children," Zoey said. She could still see the image of their kids from when she bought the flooring. She just knew that was going to happen.

Gabe feigned sarcasm. "I don't know if I want children."

"Too bad. I do, and that means you do too." She poked him in the chest with her finger.

"Anything you say, Beautiful." He rolled her over so that she was under his body.

"I like the sound of that," she whispered as his mouth met hers.

EPILOGUE

THE LONGEST WORKDAY of Gabe's life was finally over. He grabbed his bag from the passenger seat of his truck and headed into the house. Tossing the bag on the table, he hurried into the bedroom and changed out of his uniform and into jeans and a t-shirt.

Before he had time to change his socks, he heard the front door open and close. Gabe smiled to himself—Evie had sent Zoey home as he had asked. Usually, she worked for another hour after his shift ended, but he had asked Evie to send Zoey home early today. Evie had grumbled about it at first, but eventually agreed.

Heading into the living room, he saw Zoey pulling off her boots. Her hat was already gone, and her hair was windblown. Today she was wearing leggings and an oversized sweatshirt.

"Okay, I'm here. Evie said you needed me home right away. What happened?" She straightened and then smiled at him.

"It's date night," he stated, returning her smile.

He watched her flop down on the couch and lean her head back as she groaned. "No, I don't want to go to town. I'm *exhausted*, and you do not want to date this." She waved her hands over her body.

He grabbed the bag from the kitchen and sat down next to her. "We don't have to go to town for our date; I brought it home. And I love your body, Zoey."

Since moving into her seventh month of pregnancy, she had started to be more self-conscious about her body—she was a smaller woman, so she looked further along. When she had told him that they were having children, she wasn't kidding. They had married at Christmas time, and by then, she was already a few months along. It hadn't been planned, but it hadn't been totally unplanned either.

At first, he had been nervous about having a baby, but that had only lasted a few minutes as her excitement overtook his nerves. Now he marveled at how her body was changing. He was hoping for a little girl just like her mother, with red hair and spunk to match.

"I brought home Lobo Burgers, and I didn't even get into a fight." He opened the bag and handed her one.

She rolled her eyes at him. "It's not worth it if there's no fight." Zoey took the first bite of her burger, moaning as she chewed.

How had he gotten so lucky that he was married to this woman? Last year at this time, he had never wanted to get married again. Now, he couldn't imagine life without her—without her laughter every day.

After watching her enjoy her dinner for a moment, he put his burger down and said, "Do you know what today is?"

"Wednesday," Zoey said, and took another bite.

"Really! Nothing?" He asked as she chewed.

"What, am I wrong?" She asked.

"I hauled you out of Lobo last year today," he said with a smile.

"Are you sure?"

"Yep. I thought you would remember."

"I think it's tomorrow." She took another bite of her burger, chewing happily and bouncing her toes on the ground. It seemed nothing would distract her from eating.

"Nope, it's today."

Gabe watched his wife sit up and put her burger on the wrapper on the coffee table, then grab one more bite before standing up. She left him on the couch and walked into the bedroom. When she didn't come out after a few minutes, he got up and followed her into the room.

Zoey had taken off her sweatshirt and pants and was in an oversized T-shirt. She was sitting on the bed, taking off her sock, when he asked, "What are you doing?"

"I'm going to have sex with a police officer since I didn't get to last year. I thought it was tomorrow, and I planned to dress better." She threw the sock at him.

With a laugh, he walked into the room, taking off the shirt he had just put on. He gave her a mischievous look and said, "Any way I can convince you to put your uniform on?"

Smiling, she walked to the closet, pulled out her hat, and put it on. She had finally gotten it back when she had married him. "This is the only thing that fits right now or will for a long time."

He chuckled, pulling her into his arms. "Good enough." Then he kissed her until the hat fell off and neither of them noticed it was gone. Grabbing her up into his arms, she laughed as he carried her to the bed and didn't let go.

THE END

Evie falls for the boy next door in **Her Favor**

Thank you so much for reading Seeing Her Pain. Did you love it? Reviews mean everything to indie writers – you can review Seeing Her Pain on Amazon and Goodreads here!

ALSO BY ALIE GARNETT

<u>Indulge</u>

Craving Winter

Enticing Aurora

<u>Landstad, ND</u>

Invisible

Irresistible

Impulsive

Insuppressible

Intriguing

Imperfect

Irreplaceable

<u>The Great Lovely Falls</u>

Falling for the Single Mom

Falling for his Best Friends Sister

Falling for the Boss

Falling for his Step-Sister

Falling for his Fake Wife

Falling into a Second Chance

<u>Hart Series</u>

Seeing her Pain

Her Favor

Max Valentine is Looking at Me!

Keeping her Safe

<u>Stand Alone</u>

Romancing the Doctor

ABOUT ME, ALIE GARNETT

I love to read and prefer a little spice in those books. I am lucky enough to live on a small hobby farm in northern Minnesota with her husband and two kids. I enjoy spending time in the pasture with my two mini horses and one fainting goat (who doesn't actually faint). When I'm not writing, I'm busy trying to do all the things I didn't get to while writing. Or maybe I wouldn't have gotten to them anyway, because its laundry, dishes and fun things like that.